Animal Testing

M. M. Eboch, Book Editor

GREENHAVEN
PUBLISHING

Published in 2021 by Greenhaven Publishing, LLC
353 3rd Avenue, Suite 255, New York, NY 10010

Articles in Greenhaven Publishing anthologies are often edited for length to meet page requirements. In addition, original titles of these works are changed to clearly present the main thesis and to explicitly indicate the author's opinion. Every effort is made to ensure that Greenhaven Publishing accurately reflects the original intent of the authors. Every effort has been made to trace the owners of the copyrighted material.

Library of Congress Cataloging-in-Publication Data

Names: Eboch, M. M., editor.
Title: Animal testing / M. M. Eboch, book editor.
Description: First edition. | New York : Greenhaven Publishing, 2021. |
  Series: Introducing issues with opposing viewpoints | Includes
  bibliographical references and index. | Audience: Grades 7–12.
Identifiers: LCCN 2019056693 | ISBN 9781534507173 (library binding) | ISBN
  9781534507166 (paperback)
Subjects: LCSH: Animal experimentation—Juvenile literature. | Animal
  rights—Juvenile literature.
Classification: LCC HV4915 .A65 2021 | DDC 179/.4—dc23
LC record available at https://lccn.loc.gov/2019056693

Manufactured in the United States of America

Website: http://greenhavenpublishing.com

Contents

Foreword

Indulging in a wide spectrum of ideas, beliefs, and perspectives is a critical cornerstone of democracy. After all, it is often debates over differences of opinion, such as whether to legalize abortion, how to treat prisoners, or when to enact the death penalty, that shape our society and drive it forward. Such diversity of thought is frequently regarded as the hallmark of a healthy and civilized culture. As the Reverend Clifford Schutjer of the First Congregational Church in Mansfield, Ohio, declared in a 2001 sermon, "Surrounding oneself with only like-minded people, restricting what we listen to or read only to what we find agreeable is irresponsible. Refusing to entertain doubts once we make up our minds is a subtle but deadly form of arrogance." With this advice in mind, Introducing Issues with Opposing Viewpoints books aim to open readers' minds to the critically divergent views that comprise our world's most important debates.

Introducing Issues with Opposing Viewpoints simplifies for students the enormous and often overwhelming mass of material now available via print and electronic media. Collected in every volume is an array of opinions that captures the essence of a particular controversy or topic. Introducing Issues with Opposing Viewpoints books embody the spirit of nineteenth-century journalist Charles A. Dana's axiom: "Fight for your opinions, but do not believe that they contain the whole truth, or the only truth." Absorbing such contrasting opinions teaches students to analyze the strength of an argument and compare it to its opposition. From this process readers can inform and strengthen their own opinions, or be exposed to new information that will change their minds. Introducing Issues with Opposing Viewpoints is a mosaic of different voices. The authors are statesmen, pundits, academics, journalists, corporations, and ordinary people who have felt compelled to share their experiences and ideas in a public forum. Their words have been collected from newspapers, journals, books, speeches, interviews, and the Internet, the fastest growing body of opinionated material in the world.

Introducing Issues with Opposing Viewpoints shares many of the well-known features of its critically acclaimed parent series, Opposing

Viewpoints. The articles allow readers to absorb and compare divergent perspectives. Active reading questions preface each viewpoint, requiring the student to approach the material thoughtfully and carefully. Photographs, charts, and graphs supplement each article. A thorough introduction provides readers with crucial background on an issue. An annotated bibliography points the reader toward articles, books, and websites that contain additional information on the topic. An appendix of organizations to contact contains a wide variety of charities, nonprofit organizations, political groups, and private enterprises that each hold a position on the issue at hand. Finally, a comprehensive index allows readers to locate content quickly and efficiently.

Introducing Issues with Opposing Viewpoints is also significantly different from Opposing Viewpoints. As the series title implies, its presentation will help introduce students to the concept of opposing viewpoints and learn to use this material to aid in critical writing and debate. The series' four-color, accessible format makes the books attractive and inviting to readers of all levels. In addition, each viewpoint has been carefully edited to maximize a reader's understanding of the content. Short but thorough viewpoints capture the essence of an argument. A substantial, thought-provoking essay question placed at the end of each viewpoint asks the student to further investigate the issues raised in the viewpoint, compare and contrast two authors' arguments, or consider how one might go about forming an opinion on the topic at hand. Each viewpoint contains sidebars that include at-a-glance information and handy statistics. A Facts About section located in the back of the book further supplies students with relevant facts and figures.

Following in the tradition of the Opposing Viewpoints series, Greenhaven Publishing continues to provide readers with invaluable exposure to the controversial issues that shape our world. As John Stuart Mill once wrote: "The only way in which a human being can make some approach to knowing the whole of a subject is by hearing what can be said about it by persons of every variety of opinion and studying all modes in which it can be looked at by every character of mind. No wise man ever acquired his wisdom in any mode but this." It is to this principle that Introducing Issues with Opposing Viewpoints books are dedicated.

Introduction

"The history of cancer research has been the history of curing cancer in the mouse. We have cured mice of cancer for decades and it simply didn't work in human beings."
—Dr. Richard Klausner, former director
of the US National Cancer Institute

Humans have a complex relationship with animals. We keep dogs and cats as pets, beloved members of our families. Cockroaches and ants are pests that we want out of our houses. We try to save polar bears and elephants from extinction. We debate trying to eradicate all mosquitoes, because they carry diseases.

People eat many animals. Millennia ago, this meant fishing or hunting wild animals. Today, it often means raising animals on farms or ranches. Other animals provide products that we eat or drink, such as milk from cows and honey from bees. We make clothing from animal hair, fur, or skin, including wool from sheep and leather from cows. We even create new animals, breeding them for specific looks or uses. Modern cows and pigs would not exist if they hadn't been bred for food.

Animals can work for us. Horses, mules, and llamas may pull plows or carts or carry heavy loads. Dogs can do a variety of jobs, from pulling sleds to sniffing for bombs or illegal substances.

Animals also have a long history of use in medicine. Folk medicine around the world has prescribed parts of animals or animal products for a variety of diseases. Some valuable modern drugs come from animals as well. Insulin, used to treat diabetes, was originally made from the pancreas of pigs or cows, although now it is synthetic. Gelatin, which comes from the skin, bones, and cartilage of animals, is often used in capsules or coatings. Many people take supplements that come from animals, such as omega-3 fatty acids from fish oils or calcium from oyster shells.

So are animals our friends, our workers, our food, our drugs? Do we have a right to make whatever use of them we want, simply because they may benefit us? Or do animals have rights of their own?

Concern about animal welfare is not new. Some ancient religions promote a vegetarian diet, believing that killing animals is wrong. The modern animal rights movement in the United States goes back to the 1866 founding of the Humane Society. By the end of that century, the Humane Society and similar groups had organized protests against cruelty to animals. Those movements expanded in the 1900s. Protesters railed against wearing fur, dissecting frogs in classrooms, and cosmetics testing on animals.

Our connection to animals is especially complicated when it comes to research animals. Many people assume animal testing is necessary to discover new drugs and medical treatments. Most scientists, doctors, and research organizations officially support animal testing. Yet other people worry about the welfare of animals in research labs. The Animal Welfare Act, signed into law in 1966, is a US federal law that regulates the treatment of animals in research, exhibition, transport, and more. However, it does not cover many common lab animals, such as mice, rats, and birds.

Horror stories about lab animals being tortured have caused many people to rethink the necessity of using animals for research. In 1997, People for the Ethical Treatment of Animals (PETA) released an undercover video. They claimed it showed animal abuse at a research company in New Jersey. The research company argued that it followed the rules of the Animal Welfare Act. The company claimed that PETA used illegal methods and harassed scientists in attempts to shut down companies. They said the PETA videotapes had been cut and spliced in a way that was misleading. The law determined that the research company had not done anything illegal.

This was only one of many battles between animal rights organizations and animal research groups. In many cases, the research organizations had followed all laws. But to an organization such as PETA, following the law isn't enough. Nothing is enough, until all animal suffering has ceased.

On one extreme, some people believe that animals should never be killed or harmed for any reason. On another extreme, a few people dismiss animal welfare altogether. They believe that any amount of animal suffering is acceptable if humans benefit.

More moderate views argue that animal research is necessary but should be done humanely. This view says the loss of a few animals is a reasonable price to pay for improved human health. Plus, some surgical techniques and drugs developed through animal testing also benefit animals. Our pets, farm animals, and zoo conservation efforts may have benefited from animal research.

The moderate viewpoint suggests that research on animals is acceptable, as long as the animals are treated well. Most scientists conducting animal research use the "3Rs," replacement, reduction, and refinement. These guidelines are designed to reduce the use of animals in testing and to reduce animal suffering during research.

Opinion polls show that most people accept animal research, as long as the 3Rs are followed. Most doctors, scientists, and medical researchers also believe that the 3Rs do enough to protect animals. To these people, the goal is to use only a few animals in research and to make sure those animals do not suffer unnecessarily.

For other people, no level of suffering could ever be necessary. Animal welfare organizations that want to stop animal testing don't put human welfare above animal rights. They often argue that other methods of research can replace animal testing. Studies can be done using cell cultures, computer programs, or human volunteers. In many cases, these methods are as good or better than testing on animals.

However, animal research experts claim that the alternatives are not always good replacements. Testing on a live animal with all its organs and systems intact is different from testing on a few cells or using a computer model. A mouse, or even a chimpanzee, may not be a human, but it's closer than a petri dish full of cells.

Animal testing is surrounded by controversy. Is it outdated and unnecessary? Does it save lives, those of humans and other animals? Do protection laws go far enough? The current debates are explored in *Introducing Issues with Opposing Viewpoints: Animal Testing*, shedding light on this ongoing contemporary issue.

Chapter 1

Why Do We Test on Animals?

There are many reasons why scientists conduct testing on animals. But is it always necessary?

We Need Medical Trials Using Animals

Trichur Vidyasagar

"To try everything out on humans without much inkling of their effects is dangerous and therefore highly unethical."

In the following viewpoint, Trichur Vidyasagar argues that valuable medical breakthroughs often begin with animal trials. He notes that these experiments would not be allowed on human patients. Hundreds of thousands of people die each year from malaria and other diseases. Using a few hundred monkeys in animal medical experiments could save these people, according to the author. Computer models and other research methods can replace some animal experiments. Yet the author argues that in other areas, nothing adequately replaces experiments on animals. He further notes that far more animals are killed for food. Trichur Vidyasagar is a neuroscientist and professor at the University of Melbourne, Australia.

AS YOU READ, CONSIDER THE FOLLOWING QUESTIONS:
1. What are some medical breakthroughs that began with studies on monkeys?
2. Why did these medical trials start with monkeys rather than humans?
3. How are monkeys and apes different when it comes to their potential use in medical trials, according to the author?

"We Mightn't Like It, but There Are Ethical Reasons to Use Animals in Medical Research," by Trichur Vidyasagar, The Conversation, May 26, 2016. https://theconversation.com/we-mightnt-like-it-but-there-are-ethical-reasons-to-use-animals-in-medi cal-research-58878. Licensed under CC BY-ND 4.0.

The media regularly report impressive medical advances. However, in most cases, there is a reluctance by scientists, the universities, or research institutions they work for, and the media to mention animals used in that research, let alone non-human primates. Such omission misleads the public and works against long-term sustainability of a very important means of advancing knowledge about health and disease.

Consider the recent report by Ali Rezai and colleagues, in the journal Nature, of a patient with quadriplegia who was able to use his hands by just thinking about the action. The signals in the brain recorded by implanted electrodes were analysed and fed into the muscles of the arm to activate the hand directly.

When journalists report on such bionic devices, rarely is there mention of the decades of research using macaques that eventually made these early brain-machine interfaces a reality for human patients. The public is shielded from this fact, thereby lending false credence to claims by animal rights groups that medical breakthroughs come from human trials with animal experiments playing no part.

Development of such brain-machine interfaces requires detailed understanding of how the primate brain processes information and many experiments on macaques using different interfaces and computing algorithms. Human ethics committees will not let you try this on a patient until such animal research is done.

These devices are still not perfect and our understanding of brain function at a neuronal level needs more sophistication. In some cases, the macaque neural circuitry one discovers may not quite match the human's, but usually it is as close as we can get to the human scenario, needing further fine-tuning in direct human trials. However, to eliminate all animal research and try everything out on humans without much inkling of their effects is dangerous and therefore highly unethical.

The technique Dr Rezai's team used on human patients draws heavily upon work done on monkeys by many groups. This can be seen by looking at the paper and the references it cites.

Another case in point is the technique of deep brain stimulation using implanted electrodes, which is becoming an effective means of treating symptoms in many Parkinson's patients. This is now possible

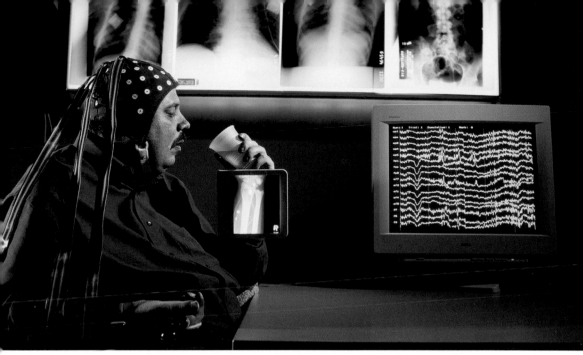

Many important medical breakthroughs, like this sensor cap that allows a quadriplegic man to drink from a glass, were first tested on animals.

largely due to the decades of work on macaques to understand in detail the complex circuitry involved in motor control. Macaques continue to be used to refine deep brain stimulation in humans.

Ethical Choices

The number of monkeys used for such long-term neuroscience experiments is relatively small, with just two used in the study above. Many more are used for understanding disease processes and developing treatment methods or vaccines in the case of infectious diseases such as malaria, Ebola, HIV/AIDS, tuberculosis and Zika.

Approximately 60,000 monkeys are used for experiments for all purposes each year in the United States, Europe and Australia.

However, if one looks at what is at stake without these experiments on non-human primates, one must acknowledge a stark reality. In many cases, the situation is similar to that which once existed with polio. Nearly 100,000 monkeys were used in the 1950s to develop the polio vaccine. Before that, millions of people worldwide, mostly children, were infected with polio every year. Around 10% died and many were left crippled.

Now, thanks to the vaccine, polio is almost eradicated.

Similarly, about 200 million people contract malaria every year, of whom 600,000 (75% being children) die, despite all efforts to control the mosquitoes that transmit the disease. Development of a vaccine is our best chance, but again primates are necessary for this, as other species are not similarly susceptible to the parasitic infection.

Circumstances are similar with other devastating ailments such as Ebola, HIV and Zika. The ethical choice is often between using a few hundred monkeys or condemning thousands or more humans to suffer or die from each one of these diseases year after year.

In the popular press and in protests against primate research, there is sometimes no distinction made between great apes (chimpanzees, bonobos and gorillas) and monkeys such as macaques, leading to misplaced emotional reactions. To my knowledge, invasive experiments on great apes are not done anywhere, because of the recognition of their cognitive proximity to humans.

While the ape and human lineages separated six million years ago, there is an additional 20 to 35 million years of evolutionary distance from monkeys, which clearly lack the sophisticated cognitive capacities of the apes.

With urgent medical issues of today such as HIV, Ebola, malaria, Zika, diabetes and neurological conditions such as stroke and Parkinson's disease, monkeys are adequate to study the basic physiology and pathology and to develop treatment methods. There is nothing extra to be gained from studying apes.

Alternatives Have Limitations

Opponents of animal research often cite the impressive developments of computer modelling, in-vitro techniques and non-invasive experiments in humans as alternatives to animal experiments. These have indeed given us great insights and are frequently used also by the very same scientists who use animals.

However, there are still critical areas where animal experimentation will be required for a long time to come.

Modelling can be done only on data already obtained and therefore can only build upon the hypotheses such data supported. The modelling also needs validation by going back to the lab to know whether the model's predictions are correct.

Real science cannot work in a virtual world. It is the synergy between computation and real experiments that advances computational research.

In-vitro studies on isolated cells from a cell line cultured in the lab or directly taken from an animal are useful alternatives. This approach is widely used in medical research. However, these cells are not the same as the complex system provided by the whole animal. Unless one delves into the physiology and pathology of various body functions and tries to understand how they relate to each other and to the environment, any insights gained from studying single cells in in-vitro systems will be limited.

Though many studies can be done non-invasively on humans and we have indeed gained much knowledge on various questions, invasive experiments on animals are necessary. In many human experiments we can study the input to the system and the output, but we are fairly limited in understanding what goes on in between. For example, interactions between diet, the microbiome, the digestive system and disease are so complex that important relationships that have to be understood to advance therapy can only be worked out in animal models.

Of course, animals are not perfect models for the human body. They can never be. Species evolve and change.

However, many parts of our bodies have remained the same over millions of years of evolution. In fact, much of our basic knowledge about how impulses are transmitted along a nerve fibre has come from studying the squid, but our understanding also gets gradually modified by more recent experiments in mammals.

Higher cognitive functions and the complex operations of the motor system have to be studied in mammals. For a small number of these studies, nothing less than a non-human primate is adequate.

The choice of species for every experiment is usually carefully considered by investigators, funding bodies and ethics committees, from both ethical and scientific viewpoints. That is why the use of non-human primates is usually a small percentage of all animals used for research. In the state of Victoria, this constitutes only 0.02%.

Medical history can vouch for the fact that the benefits from undertaking animal experiments are worth the effort in the long run and that such experimentation is sometimes the only ethical choice. Taken overall, the principle of least harm should and does prevail. There may come a day when non-invasive experiments in humans may be able to tell us almost everything that animal experiments do today, but that is probably still a long way off.

Priorities in Animal Use

The ethical pressure put on research seems to be in stark contrast to that on the food industry. It is hypocritical for a society to contemplate seriously restricting the use of the relatively small number of animals for research that could save lives when far more animals are allowed to be slaughtered just to satisfy the palate. This is despite meat being a health and environmental concern.

To put this in perspective, for every animal used in research (mostly mice, fish and rats), approximately 2,000 animals are used for food, with actual numbers varying between countries and the organisations that collect the data.

The ratio becomes even more dramatic when you consider the use of non-human primates alone. In Victoria, for every monkey used in research, more than one million animals are used for meat production. However, the monitoring of the welfare of farm animals is not in any way comparable to that which experimental animals receive.

Reduced use of livestock can greatly reduce mankind's ecological footprint and also improve our health. This is an ethical, health and environmental imperative. Animal experiments, including some on non-human primates, are also an ethical and medical imperative.

EVALUATING THE AUTHOR'S ARGUMENTS:

According to viewpoint author Trichur Vidyasagar, using monkeys for medical research is ethical because monkeys are not very closely related to humans. Do you think it matters, ethically speaking, how closely an animal is related to humans? Why or why not?

Better to Sacrifice Animals Than People

Leslie

> *"Testing on animals should be ethical because it's better to sacrifice an animal than a human."*

In the following viewpoint, a young author named Leslie offers her researched opinion on the difference between testing on animals and testing on humans. She argues that it is more ethical to test first on animals. Many medical breakthroughs have resulted from animal research. Some major medical organizations claim that animal research is important. The author argues that testing on animals is better than testing on humans, because animals have shorter lives and don't understand as much as people do. This viewpoint first appeared on Youth Voices, a platform started by teachers from the National Writing Project for youth to write about their interests.

AS YOU READ, CONSIDER THE FOLLOWING QUESTIONS:

1. What are some medical cures that have resulted from animal research, according to the viewpoint?
2. What animals are typically used for medical experiments?
3. Why does the author think it's relevant that most animals live shorter lives than humans do?

There have been a lot of people wondering is testing on animals and humans ethical? Here I would explain an opinion. Testing on animal should be ethical but testing shouldn't be ethical for humans.

Why? Testing on animals should be ethical because it's better to sacrifice an animal than a human. It's better to sacrifice an animal because they can sometimes be less used than human meaning animals are not much cared as a human. Animals must be used in cases when ethical considerations prevent the use of human subjects. When testing medicines for potential toxicity, the lives of human volunteers should not be put in danger unnecessarily. It would be unethical to perform invasive experimental procedures on human beings before the methods have been tested on animals, and some experiments involve genetic manipulation that would be unacceptable to impose on human subjects before animal testing. The World Medical Association Declaration of Helsinki states that human trials should be preceded by tests on animals. Which is why testing on humans should not be ethical. Animals are more helpful than humans while testing because it has contributed to many life-saving cures and treatments. "The California Biomedical Research Association states that nearly every medical breakthrough in the last 100 years has resulted directly from research using animals. Experiments in which dogs had their pancreases removed led directly to the discovery of insulin, critical to saving the lives of diabetics. The polio vaccine, tested on animals, reduced the global occurrence of the disease from 350,000 cases in 1988 to 27 cases in 2016. Animal research has also contributed to major advances in understanding and treating conditions such as breast cancer, brain injury, childhood leukemia, cystic fibrosis, malaria, multiple sclerosis, tuberculosis, and many others, and was instrumental in the development of pacemakers, cardiac valve substitutes, and anesthetics." Also, animals are appropriate research subjects because they are similar to human beings in many ways. "Chimpanzees share 99% of their DNA with humans, and mice are 98% genetically similar to humans. All mammals, including humans, are descended from common ancestors, and all have the same set of organs (heart, kidneys, lungs, etc.) that function in essentially the same way with the help of a bloodstream and central nervous system."

These lab rats were exposed to mobile phone radiation to test the dangers of cell phone use by humans. Conducting this testing on humans would not have been ethical. But what are the ethics of exposing animals to potentially harmful radiation?

Because animals and humans are so biologically similar, they are susceptible to many of the same conditions and illnesses, including heart disease, cancer, and diabetes. Animals often make better research subjects than human beings because of their shorter life cycles.

Testing on humans should not be ethical because most of the time humans give false-negative results and animals don't. For humans, testing can be uncomfortable and for animals they wouldn't feel uncomfortable, just scared as anyone can feel while testing. Humans have a lot more years to live. "Laboratory mice, for example, live for only two to three years, so researchers can study the effects of treatments or genetic manipulation over a whole lifespan, or across several generations, which would be infeasible using human subjects". Additionally, people might believe that animals might be treated badly while animal testing. This is wrong; animals are not treated badly they are treated with cared they are feed etc., they are in a good place. Moreover, not all animals are tested. There are only some specific animals scientist use for testing. The most common animals used in experiments around the world are non-human primates (chimpanzees in some countries, mice, rats, rabbits, guinea pigs, hamsters, birds), which are not a lot of animals. Lastly thanks to animal research, many diseases that once killed millions of people are now either treatable or curable. "Animal testing has not only benefit humans, but animals as well. Some animal testing has lead to life saving and life extending treatments for many of the animals used for testing. A complete alternative to animal testing has yet to be discovered. The focus of animal research has been characterized by three criteria, The Three R's".

In conclusion animal testing should be ethical, meaning testing on animals should happen it would be better testing on animals instead of testing on humans. Testing on humans should not be ethical.

> **FAST FACT**
>
> The World Medical Association Declaration of Helsinki requires that biomedical research involving human subjects should be based, where appropriate, on animal experimentation, but also requires that the welfare of animals used for research be respected.

Testing on animals is more helpful than testing on humans because testing on animals gives scientists more information, for example: test if the medication works, what causes something to happen, test about the health problems mostly about cancer that it's really common around the world. These are things that a human can't give you. Also, not every human gives you the correct results as animals do. Also, why focus on animal testing if it is used for a good and yet not talk about what we eat (some other people kill animals just to eat them and not for a good, as here with scientists using animals to help humans). Lastly, as said before, it's better to sacrifice an animal than a human. Some animals have less life time than humans and animals don't understand as humans do.

EVALUATING THE AUTHOR'S ARGUMENTS:

According to viewpoint author Leslie, testing on animals is more helpful than testing on humans. Does the author make a compelling case that this is true? How does the author's writing style encourage you to believe or mistrust her viewpoint?

Animal Research Can Be Humane

"For tasks that do not require animals to remain in one place, primates can be trained to voluntarily offer an arm or leg for injection or blood sampling."

Speaking of Research

In the following viewpoint, authors from Speaking of Research note that stress has physical effects on humans and other animals. Therefore, experiments on stressed animals may not be accurate. For this reason, researchers are encouraged to follow the "3Rs." These guidelines encourage researchers to treat animals humanely during tests. This can include giving them comfortable cages, proper diets, things to do, or the company of other animals. Speaking of Research is an international advocacy group. It claims to provide "accurate information about the importance of animal research in the biomedical, behavioral, and life sciences."

AS YOU READ, CONSIDER THE FOLLOWING QUESTIONS:
1. How can stress affect humans and other animals?
2. What is the pole-and-collar technique?
3. Why might animals sometimes be denied food and water before testing procedures?

When we are run down or stressed we often find ourselves more prone to getting coughs and colds. Stress changes us physiologically; it puts pressure on our autonomic nervous system, changing how drugs react inside of us. The same is true of animals.

Writing in the *Huffington Post*, Aysha Akhtar notes that when you catch a monkey with a net, it can cause much stress to the animal. She is right, and she uses this line of thinking to argue that animal research cannot produce useful results; at this point she is wrong.

What Akhtar has done is explain why the 3Rs exist. Developed by Burch and Russell in 1959[1], these principles of humane research are Refinement, Reduction and Replacement of animal research. The key "R" here is Refinement—improving the conditions of animals involved in research. This can take many forms including better diets, improved animal housing, and better training for both technicians and animals.

This training of animals is vitally important. Akhtar links to a video of monkeys being caught using a pole-and-collar technique. The pole-and-collar technique is used for a subset of studies and much time dedicated to habituating and training primates to participate in this task calmly and without stress. For example, this technique is used for those monkeys participating in behavioural and cognitive tasks that make use of neural recording. For tasks that do not require animals to remain in one place, primates can be trained (using treats) to voluntarily offer an arm or leg for injection or blood sampling. We have written about this previously, with a video featuring this training with chimpanzees in the U.S. All of this contributes to a less stressed animal that provides more accurate and reproducible data.

Akhtar makes some misleading statements about animal research and stress. For example, in a study cited by Akhtar, it is noted that mice in smaller cages developed heart defects. What she does not note from the paper is that the larger cages were enriched with a wheel, shelf and tunnel which would promote healthy living associated with fewer heart problems. Indeed the paper shows how better results can be attained from improving the environmental enrichment of animal housing.

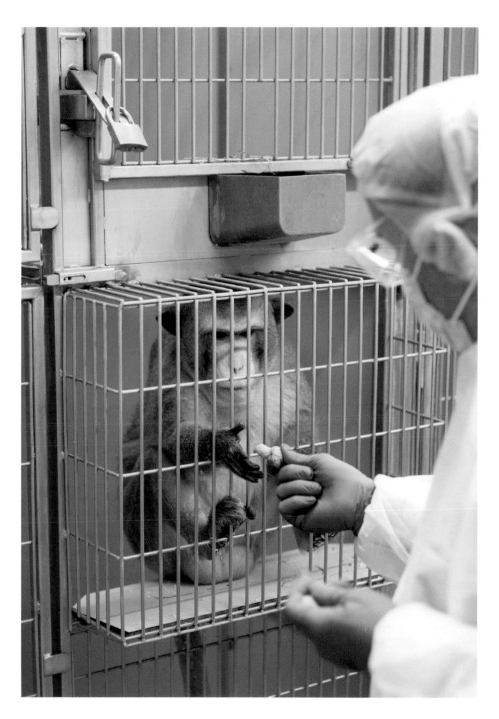

Research data from animals that have been put under stress by their treatment or living conditions may affect the validity of application to humans.

Akhtar also notes that rats can have intestinal inflammation in labs. She does not note the article says this is if they are left in "small, empty cages, with bedding if they are lucky". Such conditions are becoming increasingly uncommon, with socially housed rodents kept in larger plastic cages with bedding and enrichment designed to meet their needs.

While removing an animal from a cage can cause stress, it needn't—and perhaps Akhtar would do more good propagating good practise, as groups like the RSPCA and NC3Rs do, than trying to find new ways to attack animal research.

Claims that animals are often denied food, water and pain relief is again misleading. Food and water are sometimes denied prior to procedures, but this is in much the same way a human might be told not to eat or drink anything prior to an operation.

The fact is that Ahkthar is part of a tiny minority of scientists who try to argue animal research does not produce useful results. Perhaps, she should note *The Lancet* which wrote that

> *The use of animals in medical research and safety testing is a vital part of the quest to improve human health. It always has been and probably always will be, despite the alternatives available. Indeed, in this era of genomics and proteomics, more rather than fewer animals will be needed. Without animal testing, there will be no new drugs for new or hard-to-treat diseases.*[2]

Given that the last year has shown advances through animal research which include the first ever progeria treatment and a new diabetes treatment, Lixisenatide, it certainly seems incorrect to suggest that such methods are "fundamentally flawed".

Endnotes

1. Russell, WMS and Burch, RL. The Principles of Humane Experimental Technique. Methuen & Co Ltd.: London. 1959.

2. The Lancet, Volume 364, Issue 9437, Pages 815—816, 4 September 2004

EVALUATING THE AUTHOR'S ARGUMENTS:

In this viewpoint Speaking of Research argues that poor conditions for research animals are "increasingly uncommon." Do the authors provide evidence to support that claim? Who should be the judge of quality of life for research animals? How could the government or the public ensure that animals are treated well in research labs?

The Animal Welfare Act Helps Some Animals

National Anti-Vivisection Society

"Tens of thousands of animals are still reported to have been used for experiments involving pain or distress who did not receive any pain relief every year."

The following viewpoint looks at the Animal Welfare Act in the United States. It examines the act from its origin through the various amendments added over the years. The act has gotten stricter and covers more animals. However, some animals are excluded from these protections. In addition, the act requested reports on various concerns. Some of those reports have not yet been issued. The article also notes that research labs may not always follow the guidelines set out by the Act. The National Anti-Vivisection Society (NAVS) is a not-for-profit animal welfare organization. It is "dedicated to ending harmful, flawed and costly animal experiments through the advancement of smarter, human-relevant science."

AS YOU READ, CONSIDER THE FOLLOWING QUESTIONS:

1. What was the original purpose of the Animal Welfare Act?
2. What animals are not included in the Animal Welfare Act?
3. Does the act prevent pets from ever being sold as research animals?

The Animal Welfare Act, 7 U.S.C. 54, originally called the Laboratory Animal Welfare Act, was established in 1966 in response to growing concern for dogs and cats used in research, particularly with regard to a large number of reported thefts of dogs and cats for use in research institutions.

The U.S. Secretary of Agriculture was directed by Congress to set up a regulatory program to license dealers in dogs and cats, to register animal research facilities, and to establish humane care provisions and a system of inspections. The animals covered by this Act included live dogs, cats, monkeys (nonhuman primate mammals), guinea pigs, hamsters, and rabbits.

The Animal Welfare Act was not intended to regulate how animals are used for research purposes, but only to set standards for how they are obtained and maintained at a facility.

In order to deal with the problem of stolen pets, research facilities were required to purchase dogs and cats from licensed dealers and a system of record keeping was required for all animal dealers—both Class A breeding facilities and Class B random source dealers—and animal research facilities.

It was recognized that in order to effect changes that would prevent "pet theft" for the vivisection industry, regulations were needed for the transport, purchase, sale, housing, care, handling, and treatment of such animals.

1970 Amendments—Warm-Blooded Animals; Exhibitors; Dealers

When the Animal Welfare Act was first amended in 1970, the definition of "animal" was expanded to include warm-blooded animals generally used for research, testing, experimentation or exhibition, or as pets, but it clearly excluded farm animals, including horses, livestock and poultry. While mice, rats and birds were now presumed by many to be clearly within the coverage of the Animal Welfare Act as "warm-blooded animals," the USDA made a calculated decision to omit them when they drafted regulations to implement the law. But there will be more on that later.

Circus animals are protected under the Animal Welfare Act, but the traveling nature of the shows makes enforcement of the act difficult.

The expanded coverage now applied the Animal Welfare Act's provisions to animal exhibitors (i.e., circuses, zoos and roadside shows), and wholesale pet dealers (including breeders who sell to others under the Animal Welfare Act).

It also now required humane standards to be maintained at all times, and that animals be given the appropriate use of pain-killing drugs, if that did not interfere with the research—although this is an exception that is widely invoked. Tens of thousands of animals are still reported to have been used for experiments involving pain or distress who did not receive any pain relief every year. The USDA was again directed to develop regulations to implement these provisions.

1976 Amendments—Transportation, Handling, Fighting

In 1976, the Animal Welfare Act was again amended, this time to include transportation carriers and intermediate handlers of animals under its provisions.

The new law also made it a crime to sponsor or promote fighting between live birds, dogs or other mammals in interstate commerce, and the use of civil fines for violations was instituted.

1985 Amendments—IACUCs, Psychological Enrichment

In 1985, additional amendments were made that focused almost entirely on the issue of animals used in research. A minimum standard of care was stated with more specificity and animal research facilities were required to create Institutional Animal Care and Use Committees (IACUCs), which include the presence of a member of the public from outside the facility. This is the first time the Animal Welfare Act addressed what was being done with animals as research subjects, requiring institutional oversight and approval of each experiment—and requiring that researchers justify how the animals are being used, as well as the number and species used.

Other major changes that were sought by the animal protection community were a provision that dogs held by research facilities be exercised and a requirement that research facilities provide "a physical environment adequate to promote the psychological well-being of primates." This represented the first time that Congress had extended the concern and scope of the law beyond certain obvious requirements such as the provision of food and water.

1990 Amendments—Pet Protection Act

The next round of amendments to the Animal Welfare Act came in 1990 and was concerned primarily with the treatment of cats and dogs. Government entities, state or municipal pounds or shelters, private shelters, and federal research facilities were now required to hold dogs and cats for not less than five days to enable owners to reclaim their lost pets or to allow shelters an opportunity to adopt out individual animals before selling a dog or cat to a dealer.

It also addressed the continuing problem of Class B, or random source, animal dealers by requiring the dealer to provide the recipient with a valid certification including a detailed description of the animal and the source from which it was obtained. A statement was also required from the provider of the animals that they knew that the dog or cat may be used for research when they released it to the Class B dealer.

2002 Amendments—Mice, Rats and Birds Excluded

In 2002, a brief amendment to the Animal Welfare Act was included as part of an Agricultural Appropriations Bill, which "excludes (1) birds, rats of the genus Rattus, and mice of the genus Mus, bred for use in research, from coverage under the Act."

But it also required a report on the use of mice, rats and birds, that was to be compiled by the National Research Council and submitted within one year to the Committee on Agriculture of the House of Representatives and the Committee on Agriculture, Nutrition, and Forestry of the Senate on the implications of including rats, mice, and birds within the definition of animal under the regulations promulgated under the Animal Welfare Act. This detailed report was to include: the number and types of entities that use rats, mice, and birds for research purposes; which agencies regulate their use; an estimate of the additional costs likely to be incurred by breeders and research facilities resulting from the additional regulatory requirements needed in order to afford the same level of protection to rats, mice, and birds as is provided for species regulated by the Department of Agriculture; and recommendations as to how to minimize any additional costs.

No report has yet been issued.

2008 Amendments Under the Farm Bill

Every five years a massive reconsideration of agricultural policies, regulations and appropriations is conducted by Congress. Dubbed "the Farm Bill," this mammoth legislation always starts out with multiple animal protective measures, but history has shown that this is NOT a sympathetic forum for animal protection/welfare measures.

The 2008 bill was no exception. The Senate version of the bill included amendments that would have delayed the introduction of cloned animal products into the marketplace; incorporated provisions from the Human and Pet Food Safety bills; and would have ended the use of random source animals for research.

The bill as passed by the House would have prohibited both the use of live animals for demonstrations to market medical devices and ended the use of animals from Class B dealers (random source animals).

What actually passed into law was a prohibition on the importation of live dogs under the age of 6 months, (with exceptions) and increased fines for violations under the Animal Welfare Act to $10,000 per violation (previously $2,500).

A panel was also created to look at any independent reviews conducted by a nationally recognized panel of experts on the use of Class B dogs and cats in federally-supported research. This panel was charged with looking at existing studies to determine how frequently such dogs and cats are used in research by the National Institutes of Health and to make recommendations outlining the parameters of such use that can be applied within the Department of Agriculture.

This report, issued by the National Academies of Science, concluded that although "random source dogs and cats may be desirable and necessary for certain types of biomedical research, it is not necessary to acquire them through Class B dealers."

Summary of AWA Protections

In short, the Animal Welfare Act covers many commercial uses of many animals, creating a regulatory network administered by the U.S. Department of Agriculture.

- Permits are required to buy and sell listed animals or register for their use by dealers of animals, exhibitors of animals, and research facilities that use listed animals, but pet owners, agricultural use and retail pet stores are exempted from the provisions of this federal law.

- There are limitations/regulations on how animals may enter the controlled chain of commerce, to eliminate the use of stolen animals.
- There are limitations/regulations on the environmental conditions under which the animals must be kept.
- Research facilities may purchase listed animals only from licensed dealers.
- Those who transport the listed animals must comply with published regulations governing the well-being of the animals.
- Research facilities must create an Animal Care Committee to review the use of animals by the facility and inspect the animal housing facilities.
- Research facilities must abide by legal restrictions on the imposition of pain during research.
- Research facilities must comply with extensive regulations concerning the housing and care of animals used in research.
- In a separate provision, it made it illegal for any person to knowingly sponsor or exhibit an animal in any animal fighting venture to which any animal was moved in interstate or foreign commerce.

The provisions of the Animal Welfare Act are enforced by the U.S. Department of Agriculture (USDA), which enacted regulations to implement these provisions. The USDA's Animal and Plant Health Inspection Service (APHIS) conducts annual inspections of all licensed facilities and generally oversees compliance.

EVALUATING THE AUTHOR'S ARGUMENTS:

In this viewpoint, authors from the National Anti-Vivisection Society describe many of the details of the Animal Welfare Act. Do the viewpoint authors appear to have an opinion on the act? If so, what is that opinion, and how could you tell?

In Vitro Tests Are Not Enough

"Cells artificially cultured outside the body are in a much more sensitive situation when it comes to exposure to chemical agents."

David Tribe

In the following viewpoint, David Tribe discusses in vitro testing done on cells growing in petri dishes. This method is easier than using animals for medical research. It avoids the ethical questions in animal research. However, the author argues, in vitro testing is not an adequate replacement for tests on living, complex bodies. As an example, the article discusses in vitro tests that suggested autism was caused by a chemical used in some vaccines. Later tests found these conclusions to be false. The author uses this example to show that in vitro tests are not, by themselves, adequate for medical research. David Tribe is a professor at the University of Melbourne. He also writes for Biology Fortified, a nonprofit organization focused on biotechnology.

AS YOU READ, CONSIDER THE FOLLOWING QUESTIONS:

1. What does in vitro mean?
2. How did in vitro tests lead to a wrong claim about the cause of autism?
3. What effect did this wrong claim have on the rates of vaccine use?

A nswers to the wrong questions.

The moral message of this short story, taken from Paul Offit's inspiring *Autism's False Prophets*, is that fuzzy thinking about biology and human health can easily lead people and activist movements to do well intentioned, but tragically dangerous and stupid things.

> *Lyn Redwood is a nurse practitioner who lives in Atlanta, Georgia. By the time her third child, Will, was born, she had been a medical professional for twenty years. "My son Will weighed in at close to nine pounds at birth," she said. "He was a happy baby who ate and slept well, smiled, cooed, walked, and talked all by one year of age." But after his first birthday, Will began to change. "He lost speech, eye contact, and suffered intermittent bouts of diarrhea, [then he was] diagnosed with pervasive developmental delay, a form of autism." When the AAP issued its press release in July 1999 urging the immediate removal of thimerosal from vaccines, Redwood called her doctor's office. "I reviewed [Will's] vaccine record and my worst fears were confirmed," she said. "All of his early vaccines that could have possibly contained thimerosal, had." Redwood believed she had found the cause of her son's autism.*

Paul Offit goes on to describe how, in the 2000s, the mercury containing vaccine preservative thimerosal was viewed as the cause of autism by some scientists, and by many parents, such as distraught parents like Lyn Redwood who were entangled in the very trying circumstances of their own child having the behavioural patterns of autism.

In vitro means artificial biology out of the body.

Simplification is a very powerful way of making scientific progress in biology, because intact biological systems, such as people and human communities are very complicated. Around the year 2004, a simplified scientific method led to thimerosal chemical (which is a preservative that is added to vaccines) being fingered as the cause of the developmental disorder autism in children.

One part of this simplified approach was—rather than directly testing the effects of thimerosal on intact whole animals or people — to test the chemical for effect on living organism human cell components separated away of the body. This involves doing experiments involving mercury or thimerosal exposure to artificially cultured living human cells proliferating as artificial thin layers of tissue growing in Petri dishes.

This in vitro investigation method is easier than doing more expensive, complicated and ethically difficult studies on humans themselves as whole living organism's, and simpler even more than directly investigating what's happening with real human disease in populations of living people who suffer actual health problems.

But in interpreting the outcomes of these experiments it is important to bear in mind that cells artificially cultured outside the body are in a much more sensitive situation when it comes to exposure to chemical agents. The normal protective barriers of skin and intestinal layers and blood brain barriers are absent, excretion systems such as the kidney are missing, and doses of chemicals in in vitro tests can be unrealistically high compared to what dose will appear inside the body in a real-life situation.

The dose makes the poison.

The dose of chemical to which the potential target of chemical damage is exposed is always a crucial factor in determining whether any toxic effects on the body will happen. The dose makes the poison, and in fact everyone of us is exposed every day to very low doses of mercury, but we don't all suffer from mercury poisoning.

It's always important in biology to ask "What happens inside the living organism—in vivo?" A simplified "in vitro" approach can give you answers, but when you do investigations away from the living organism you always should check rigorously to see whether the simplified system is giving answers to the wrong questions.

For some studies, there is no substitute for testing cells on a live subject.

Science-in-reverse can get you into trouble, and put the cart before the horse

Paul Offit uses the expression "science-in-reverse" to explain how simplified biological experiments can give misleading answers about causes of autism. He's referring to the logical trap of jumping the gun, and using "in vitro" experiments with isolated component of the human body exposed to mercury compounds in Petri dishes to formulate a presumptive mechanism for how the disease occurs, before checking carefully and conclusively that exposure to mercury compound in a living human actually does cause autism.

The crucial problem with this science-in-reverse is that microscopic behaviour of a body component in an artificially devised system may be irrelevant to the real disease process. Answers can be found, but they are misleading answers because the wrong questions are being posed. It's putting the cart before the horse.

In a later passage of the book to that given above, Paul Offit relates how this presumed mechanism-based microscopic dissection approach—science-in-reverse—seemed in the year 2004 to be giving answers to what causes autism:

... Boyd Haley, a professor and chairman of the department of chemistry at the University of Kentucky, was a superb researcher who had published several papers in the Proceedings of the National Academy of Sciences—a publication of the National Academy of Sciences and a highly respected scientific journal internationally. Haley proposed that tubulin, a protein in cells necessary for their movement, was damaged by thimerosal. "Inhibit tubulin function with thimerosal injections," he said, "and you inhibit the immune response {causing autism}." Lyn Redwood [as an anti-vaccine activist] was happy to have Boyd Haley on her side. "He understands the levels of exposure that our infants received," she said. "That's why Dr. Haley is such a wonderful advocate for us. He reads the science and understands it."

Soon Boyd Haley was joined by another biochemist: Richard Deth, a professor of biochemistry at Northeastern University in Boston. In 2004, Deth had written a paper published in Molecular Psychiatry that weighed in on the thimerosal debate. Using nerve cells grown in laboratory flasks, Deth had found that thimerosal inhibited an important metabolic pathway. He reasoned that some children were probably better able to use this pathway to excrete mercury, and to avoid its toxic effects, thanothers. And, like the Geiers, Deth believed he had found a cure. Testifying before Dan Burton's Committee on Government Reform, Deth said, "The good news that goes along with this [knowledge] is that metabolic interventions are proving to be effective for autism. These treatments include [vitamin] B12 itself, which can produce dramatic improvements in some kids. Giving B12 turns out to be an antidote for [mercury]." Richard Deth believed he had found a cause (alteration in cellular metabolism) and a treatment (vitamin B12) for autism.

The big problem with this line of argument is that it was an illusion, because thimerosal in vaccines was not the cause of autism.

The encouraging findings in the quoted passage just above were indeed answers to the wrong questions. Subsequent investigations, and the well documented experiences of countries which withdrew thimerosal preservative from vaccines, found that autism rates continue to rise even without any thimerosal in vaccines, proving conclusively that there was no connection between presence of thimerosal in vaccines and development of autism in children. In fact, vaccines don't cause autism.

But chasing after the wrong explanation of autism—science-in-reverse—not only gave us the wrong answers about biology, it was also dangerous because it suggested treatments for autism which are not only useless, but harmful. And many people were exposed to these dangerous treatments, as described vividly and comprehensively in *Autism's False Prophets* and other books about the anti-vaccination tragedies of recent years. Worse still, wrong answers about thimerosal added to general parental confusion about whether vaccines were safe, and vaccination rates fell in many communities in the USA and Europe, leading to many cases of unnecessary disease and tragic death from vaccine preventable disease.

It is important to get the scientific method right when people's lives and health are at stake. Autism's False Prophets shows why bad science, risky medicine, and the search for a cure can be dangerous.

EVALUATING THE AUTHOR'S ARGUMENTS:

In this viewpoint, David Tribe argues that in vitro tests are not a replacement for tests conducted on living, complex bodies. Does the example the author provided convince you that this is true? The author does not directly address animal tests. Could his point lead to the conclusion that animal tests are necessary? Why or why not?

Chapter 2

Is Animal Testing Wrong?

Some animal advocacy groups have broken into labs and freed the animals.

Viewpoint

1

Animal Testing Doesn't Work

People for the Ethical Treatment of Animals

"The problem is that [animal testing] hasn't worked, and it's time we stopped dancing around the problem."

In the following viewpoint, People for the Ethical Treatment of Animals (PETA) argues that animal testing is useless as well as cruel. The authors list some other methods of medical research and claim these tests are often cheaper and faster than animal research. In addition, they argue, results of such tests don't suffer from differences between humans and animal research subjects. Some of these methods use human cells or tissues. Others rely on computer models. Finally, research can be conducted on human volunteers in some cases. For medical training, the article says that artificial humans work better than practicing surgery techniques on animals. PETA is the world's largest animal rights organization.

AS YOU READ, CONSIDER THE FOLLOWING QUESTIONS:

1. Why have animal experiments been a failure, according to the authors?
2. What are other options for medical research besides animal experiments?
3. What is a human-patient simulator?

"Alternatives to Animal Testing," People for the Ethical Treatment of Animals, Inc. ("PETA"). Reprinted by Permission.

During a government meeting about funding for research, former U.S. National Institutes of Health director Dr. Elias Zerhouni admitted to his colleagues that experimenting on animals to help humans has been a major failure:

> We have moved away from studying human disease in humans. … We all drank the Kool-Aid on that one, me included. … The problem is that [animal testing] hasn't worked, and it's time we stopped dancing around the problem. … We need to refocus and adapt new methodologies for use in humans to understand disease biology in humans.

Today—because experiments on animals are cruel, expensive, and generally inapplicable to humans—the world's most forward-thinking scientists have moved on to develop and use methods for studying diseases and testing products that replace animals and are actually relevant to human health. These alternatives to animal testing include sophisticated tests using human cells and tissues (also known as in vitro methods), advanced computer-modeling techniques (often referred to as in silico models), and studies with human volunteers. These and other non-animal methods are not hindered by species differences that make applying animal test results to humans difficult or impossible, and they usually take less time and money to complete.

These and other non-animal methods are not hindered by species differences that make applying animal test results to humans difficult or impossible, and they usually take less time and money to complete. PETA and its affiliates fund the development of many of these alternatives to animal testing, vigorously promote their use to governments and companies around the world, and publish research on their superiority to traditional animal tests.

Here are just a few examples of the numerous state-of-the-art, non-animal research methods available and their demonstrated benefits:

In Vitro Testing

- Harvard's Wyss Institute has created "organs-on-chips" that contain human cells grown in a state-of-the-art system to mimic

Animal rights groups believe that modern science has enough viable alternatives to using animals for testing.

the structure and function of human organs and organ systems. The chips can be used instead of animals in disease research, drug testing, and toxicity testing and have been shown to replicate human physiology, diseases, and drug responses more accurately than crude animal experiments do. Some companies, such as the HμRel Corporation, have already turned these chips into products that other researchers can use in place of animals.

- A variety of cell-based tests and tissue models can be used to assess the safety of drugs, chemicals, cosmetics, and consumer products. CeeTox (now owned by Cyprotex) developed a method to assess the potential of a substance to cause a skin allergy in humans that incorporates MatTek's EpiDerm™ Tissue Model—a 3-dimensional, human cell–derived skin model that replicates key traits of normal human skin. It replaces tests in which experimenters injected guinea pigs or mice with a substance or applied it to their shaved skin to determine an allergic response. MatTek's EpiDerm™ is also being used to replace rabbits in painful, prolonged experiments that have traditionally been used to evaluate chemicals for their ability to corrode or irritate the skin.

- Devices made by German-based manufacturer VITROCELL are used to expose human lung cells in a dish to chemicals in order to test the health effects of inhaled substances. Every day, humans inhale numerous chemicals—some intentionally (such as cigarette smoke) and some inadvertently (such as pesticides). Using the VITROCELL machines, human cells are exposed to the airborne chemical on one side while receiving nutrients from a blood-like liquid on the other—mimicking what actually occurs when a chemical enters a human lung. These devices replace the current method of forcing rats into tiny tubes and making them inhale toxic substances for hours before finally killing them.
- Researchers at the European Union Reference Laboratory for alternatives to animal testing developed five different tests that use human blood cells to detect contaminants in drugs that cause a potentially dangerous fever response when they enter the body. The non-animal methods replace the crude use of rabbits in this painful procedure.

Computer (*in silico*) Modeling

- Researchers have developed a wide range of sophisticated computer models that simulate human biology and the progression of developing diseases. Studies show that these models can accurately predict the ways that new drugs will react in the human body and replace the use of animals in exploratory research and many standard drug tests.
- Quantitative structure-activity relationships (QSARs) are computer-based techniques that can replace animal tests by making sophisticated estimates of a substance's likelihood of being hazardous, based on its similarity to existing substances and our knowledge of human biology. Companies and governments are increasingly using QSAR tools to avoid animal testing of chemicals, and PETA actively promotes and funds their use internationally.

Research with Human Volunteers

• A method called "microdosing" can provide vital information on the safety of an experimental drug and how it is metabolized in humans prior to large-scale human trials. Volunteers are given an extremely small one-time drug dose, and sophisticated imaging techniques are used to monitor how the drug behaves in the body. Microdosing can replace certain tests on animals and help screen out drug compounds that won't work in humans so that they won't needlessly advance to government-required animal testing.

• Advanced brain imaging and recording techniques—such as functional magnetic resonance imaging (fMRI)—with human volunteers can be used to replace archaic experiments in which rats, cats, and monkeys have their brains damaged. These modern techniques allow the human brain to be safely studied down to the level of a single neuron (as in the case of intracranial electroencephalography), and researchers can even temporarily and reversibly induce brain disorders using transcranial magnetic stimulation.

Human-Patient Simulators

• Strikingly lifelike computerized human-patient simulators that breathe, bleed, convulse, talk, and even "die" have been shown to teach students physiology and pharmacology better than crude exercises that involve cutting up animals. The most high-tech simulators mimic illnesses and injuries and give the appropriate biological response to medical interventions and medication injections. All medical schools across the U.S., Canada, and India have completely replaced the use of animal laboratories in medical training with simulators as well as virtual reality systems, computer simulators, and supervised clinical experience.

- For more advanced medical training, systems like TraumaMan—which replicates a breathing, bleeding human torso and has realistic layers of skin and tissue, ribs, and internal organs—are widely used to teach emergency surgical procedures and have been shown in numerous studies to impart lifesaving skills better than courses that require students to cut into live pigs, goats, or dogs.

Visit the PETA International Science Consortium Ltd. website (http://www.piscltd.org.uk) for more information on the global work of PETA and its affiliates to promote the development and use of modern, non-animal research and testing methods. A list of alternative toxicity testing methods approved by regulators can be found here (https://www.piscltd.org.uk/alternatives/), and a list of companies and organizations involved in the development of non-animal methods can be found here (https://www.piscltd.org.uk/links-resources/).

EVALUATING THE AUTHOR'S ARGUMENTS:

In this viewpoint, PETA argues that experiments on animals are not necessary, because we have alternatives. Compare this to Chapter 1, Viewpoint 5, which claims in vitro tests are not enough. Does this viewpoint adequately address the concerns of the previous one? Can you think of other concerns when it comes to replacing all animal testing?

Animal Experiments Cause Harm

Humane Research Australia

"Extrapolation from animals to humans can and does result in dangerously misleading outcomes."

In the following viewpoint, Humane Research Australia discusses failures and problems with animal research. It argues that humans are too different from other animals. Therefore, results from animal tests won't be accurate in humans. In addition, medical research often starts by causing diseases in animals. Intentionally giving subjects a disease may skew the study results. The authors list several drugs that were approved after animal testing and later turned out to be harmful. They also list medical achievements made without animal tests. Finally, the authors argue that even successful animal tests were not necessary. Some breakthroughs attributed to animal testing were really made, or could have been made, without it. Humane Research Australia is a nonprofit organization opposed to animal experiments.

AS YOU READ, CONSIDER THE FOLLOWING QUESTIONS:

1. How do species differences affect animal testing, according to the viewpoint?
2. Why are some "successful" animal experiments misleading, according to the authors?
3. Why does animal testing continue, according to the viewpoint?

"Medical Research," by Humane Research Australia, December 2010. Reprinted by permission.

R esearchers cite a number of examples of which they consider the use of animals to be integral. However they do not provide any measure of how the perceived "successes" compare with the number of delays and disasters animal use has caused throughout history.

Did you know, for example:

- 85% of drugs that reach clinical trial fail to attain general distribution (which certainly questions the efficacy of animal tests).
- The development of the Polio vaccine, often cited by researchers as an example of the necessity of animal experiments, was long delayed due to misleading results from primate experiments. This was stated under oath by Dr Sabin (inventor of the polio vaccine).
- Penicillin was delayed for 15 years and blood transfusions for more than a century.

We are constantly reading news headlines that breakthroughs have been made in the cure against cancer yet today it remains one of the greatest killers in the Western world. What we don't hear are the many drugs that are recalled on a regular basis—drugs that have been "successfully" tested on animals and have later proven to be dangerous to human health.

History

The concept of medical research was fathered by Hippocrates whose methodology was to predict the course of disease through clinical observation. In second century Rome however, Galen—a revered physician put Hippocrates' human-based research off course when he began cutting into goats, pigs and monkeys due to a Church protocol disallowing human autopsies. His theories were therefore based on a combination of his findings through vivisection and observation of humans and proved to be very inaccurate.

Belgian anatomist and physician, Andreas Vesalius, resumed work on human dissections in 1543 and discovered that most of Galen's discoveries were erroneous and published his findings in De Corporis Humani Fabrica (Structure of the Human Body). With such information the scientific community overpowered the Church's objections

In the 1960s, many doctors prescribed thalidomide to treat morning sickness in pregnant women. Later, the drug was found to be the cause of limb deformities in approximately 10,000 children. Could this have been avoided if the drug had first been tested on animals?

and dissection of human bodies continued, leading to a great acceleration of medical knowledge.

In the mid nineteenth century, French physiologist Claude Bernard reinstigated animal experiments by convincing the scientific community that if a disease could not be replicated in animals it could not exist (despite clinical evidence to the contrary). It became understood amongst scientists that animal experimentation could provide both money and reputation (regardless of its misleading results).

The situation remains the same today.

Species Differences

Extrapolation from animals to humans can and does result in dangerously misleading outcomes. The reason is due to species differences. Different species have a different genetic make-up and it is on the genetic and molecular level that variances occur. Results can differ between different sexes of the same species, different strains, and even due to different housing conditions or levels of stress within the same species. So if such differences can occur within the same species then it's negligent to extrapolate from say a rat to a human—two totally different species with a totally different genetic make-up. Researchers often claim that animals are used because they need to test in a living system rather than on isolated cells or tissue, however an entire living system creates more variables which can further affect the outcome of any results.

Another problem is that quite often a disease that is being researched does not appear in its natural state but instead is artificially induced in the research animal. This can result in the same symptoms being expressed but the underlying illness is not the same as in its human form. Researchers then try to cure the symptoms of the falsified illness but do not address nor cure the real problem, which may have been caused, or further affected, by social and environmental factors rather than biological factors alone.

Even animal-researcher and former director of Wellcome Research Laboratories, Dr Miles Weatherall admitted: "Every species has its own metabolic pattern, and no two species are likely to metabolise a drug identically."

Some examples of "species differences" are:

- Morphine sedates man but stimulates cats;
- Aspirin causes birth defects in rats and mice but not in humans;
- Penicillin is highly toxic for guinea pigs and hamsters; and
- The common industrial chemical benzene causes leukemia in man but not in mice.

Examples of Failures

By looking through medical history we see many examples of how progress has been made without the use of animals, how progress has been retarded due to animal-based research and how disasters have occurred because of it. The use of the following drugs/procedures were delayed for many years due to the misleading conclusions from animal-based research:

Penicillin: Discovered by Fleming in 1928 who found that bacteria would not grow on a culture medium accidentally contaminated by a mould. Even before this discovery however, mould on damp cheeses were used to make a plaster for infected wounds. Fleming lost interest in his discovery when a sample was injected into rabbits and became deactivated by blood.

Many years later, the drug was resurrected by Oxford scientists Florey and Chain. Fleming wished to inject penicillin into the spine of a dangerously ill patient but the results of the administration were unknown. Florey tried the experiment on a cat, but due to a shortage of time it was also administered to the patient before the results of the cat test were available. The cat died, however the patient's health improved.

Blood Transfusions: Following the discovery of blood circulation in 1666, Richard Lower transferred blood from one dog to another. A year later, French physician Jean Denis transfused lambs blood into a boy. After a number of patients died following the procedure, and a lawsuit brought against the Professor, no further attempts were made for more than a century. It wasn't until the early part of the nineteenth century that it was realised that transfusions could only be sourced from human donors, and the method only became safe after the discovery of the main blood groups by Karl Landsteiner in 1900. The discovery was made by mixing human blood in test tubes and not through the use of animals.

Digitalis: The beneficial effects of digitalis for the treatment of heart conditions were known for many years however its widespread use was delayed because animal experiments indicated a dangerous rise in blood pressure.

Iron Sorbitol: Used as a treatment for iron deficiency anaemia. It was originally injected into the muscles of rats and rabbits and found to cause sarcomas at the site of injection. 20 years after the initial research on rats it revealed no real hazard during clinical experience.

The following drugs were all "successfully" tested on animals, yet produced widespread damage when applied to humans:

Thalidomide: Probably the most infamous drug disaster, marketed in 1957 by Chemie Grunenthal, and in 1958 by the Distillers Company, as a sedative and to treat morning sickness in pregnant women. Initially, it caused peripheral neuritis—numbness and cold, severe muscular cramps, weakness of the limbs and lack of coordination. In the following years it was found to cause damage to the human fetus, resulting in around 10,000 children born crippled and deformed with missing limbs.

[Note: Researchers often cite Thalidomide as a strong argument of why animal experiments ARE necessary, because if it had it been tested on pregnant animals we would have seen birth malformations (teratogenicity). However this is not a convincing argument. After thousands of malformed babies were born researchers started conducting teratogenicity tests and failed to produce similar malformations in numerable other species].

Finally, the White New Zealand rabbit also gave birth to deformed offspring, but only at a dose between 25 to 300 times that given to humans. It also eventually occurred in monkeys, but only at ten times the normal dose. The bottom line is that more animal testing would not have found the side effects, and even if they had tested on the White New Zealand rabbit, Thalidomide would still have gone to market since the vast majority of species showed no ill effect. It is only possible to produce specific deformities in specific species, and chances are the right species would never have been used.

Clioquinol: The main ingredient in Ciba Geigy's anti-diarrhoea drugs caused an epidemic of disease in Japan in the 1960s. It was banned in Japan in 1970 and then removed from the world market in 1982 (12 years later!). At least 10,000 people, and possibly up to 30,000, fell victim to SMON (subacute myelo-optic neuropathy), a disease which causes numbness, weakness in the legs, paralysis, eye problems including blindness, all due to nerve damage.

Eraldin: Marketed by ICI in the 1970s for the treatment of heart conditions it was thoroughly tested on animals which gave no indication of the tragedy it would cause. It was withdrawn in 1976 after it was found to cause serious eye damage, including blindness, and 23 deaths. Over 1,000 patients received compensation for the damage it caused.

Isoprenaline aerosol inhalers: During the 1960s at least 3,500 young British asthma sufferers died following its use.

Opren: An arthritis drug introduced in 1980 by Eli Lilly after safely passing animal tests. It was withdrawn in August 1982 after being found to be highly toxic in humans, with 3,500 reports of harmful effects including 61 British deaths, mainly through liver damage in the elderly.

Zomax: An anti-inflammatory drug marketed in 1980 to treat postoperative pain. It was withdrawn in 1983 after deaths from severe allergic reactions.

Osmosin: A slow release drug to treat arthritis caused 40 deaths in the UK alone and was withdrawn in 1983 after only ten months.

Zelmid: Anti-depressant drug marketed by Astra in 1982. Withdrawn in 1983 after 300 reports of adverse reactions, including convulsions, liver damage, neuropathies and Guillain-Barre syndrome.

Anti-inflammatory drugs **phenylbutazone** and **oxyphenbutazone** are responsible for an estimated 10,000 deaths worldwide.

Premarin: In July 2002, over nine million women worldwide who had been prescribed Premarin as a hormone replacement therapy were advised that it has been found to greatly increase the risk of breast cancer, heart disease, strokes and blood clots in the lungs. Premarin was introduced in 1942 by Wyeth-Ayerst and is one of the most prescribed drugs in the United States. In Australia, 300,000 women have been urged to seek advice from their doctor.

VIOXX: Recalled in September 2004. It's a medication for arthritis and has now been found to increase the risk of heart attack and stroke.

This list is by no means exhaustive. It merely serves as a snapshot to illustrate how dangerously misleading the use of non-human animals can be in medical research when results are applied to human conditions.

Examples of Successes Without the Use of Animals

The following significant advances in medical progress have all been achieved without the use of non-human animals:

Sanitation: In the mid to late 19th Century, death rates fell dramatically due to the decline in infectious diseases, including TB, bronchitis, pneumonia, influenza, whooping cough, measles, scarlet fever, diptheria, smallpox, cholera, typhoid, diarrhoea and dysentry. However the mortality for each of these infections were declining long before the introduction of antibiotics and immunization. Instead they have been linked to public health measures and social legislation that have improved the living standards of working people, and to better understanding and availability of nutritional requirements.

Surgery: Particularly for wounds of the heart and chest during the Second World War became a common procedure, providing opportunity for many fundamental skills of heart surgery to be developed.

Lawson Tait has been recognised as one of the most brilliant surgeons in history and pioneered many of our present day surgical techniques. He was also a fierce critic of animal research. He was the first to successfully perform a cholecystectomy (gall bladder operation), removal of the appendix, operation on a case of ruptured ectopic pregnancy, and many abdominal operations. He was also a strong proponent of cleanliness during surgery, which during his time was not a common practice.

Anaesthesia: Before the discovery of anaesthetics, the best surgeons were those who could perform painful operations in the shortest possible time. The introduction of anaesthesia was therefore considered to be a huge medical advance.

In the 1840's, laughing gas parties and "ether frolics" were popular entertainments amongst medical students. It was the recreational inhalation of ether that prompted Dr Crawford Long to suggest its use for surgical procedures. Further "partying" led to the discovery of the properties of chloroform and others.

X-rays: Discovered by accident in 1895 by physics professor Wilhelm Rontgen. He was passing electrical discharges through a partially evacuated glass tube when he discovered by accident that highly penetrative but invisible rays were emitted from the tube. By putting his own hand in the path of the rays he learned that flesh, but not bones, was transparent to the rays.

When Animal Research DOES Work

Advances which have been claimed to have been made through the use of animals could have been made through other means. Additionally, many discoveries were made by non-animal methods; later experiments on animals only further verified these breakthroughs as being correct, giving false credit to the use of animals.

William Harvey for example, has been credited as being the first to provide an accurate description of the blood's circulation in the 1600's (although it has been reported that the Chinese understood the blood's action as early as 2650 B.C.E.). However Dr Lawson Tait (one of the most famous surgeons of the nineteenth century responded: "That he [Harvey] made any contribution to the facts of the [blood circulation] case by vivisection is conclusively disproved. ... It is, more-over, perfectly clear that were it incumbent on anyone to prove the circulation of the blood as a new theme, it could not be done by any vivisectional process but could, at once, be satisfactorily established by a dead body and an injecting syringe."

Ovarian function was demonstrated by physician Dr. Robert T. Morris in 1895 in surgical procedures on women, yet history credits the discovery to Emil Knauer who reproduced the procedure in rabbits in 1896.

Banting and Best are often cited as having discovered insulin through animal experiments in 1922. However further investigation of the history of diabetes reveals that this is not the case. The discovery of insulin dates back to 1788 when an English physician, Thomas Cawley, performed an autopsy on a diabetic. Unfortunately subsequent research on animals delayed the acceptance of his hypothesis. Despite the existence of insulin already being well known, it was evidence obtained from Banting and Best's dog experiments that was the convincing factor for scientists. It seems that all too often researchers insist on animal experiments in an attempt to verify any discovery, however the use of animals to further work does not change the fact that a technique or discovery was made without animals.

"Historically, vivisection has been much like a slot machine. If researchers pull the experimentation lever often enough, eventually some benefits will result by pure chance." Dr John McArdle, Animals Agenda, March 1988.

Such logic however, does NOT constitute good science.

Why It Continues

There are many reasons that vivisection still occurs. Primarily it is due to the many vested interests attached to its continuation. There are many businesses that thrive from breeding lab animals with specific traits, manufacturing housing systems, and of course the pharmaceutical companies that want quick results—despite these results often providing misleading information that has led to drug recalls.

Another reason is for academic recognition. Using animals can be a quick and easy way to get scientific papers published, and of course the greater "credibility" (through producing papers) the more chance of receiving government and public grants to continue more animal research.

Unfortunately researchers who use animals are seldom questioned about their methodology and the public are denied access to knowing what happens to animals, nor how inaccurate the results can be when extrapolated to humans. They therefore continue their practices as the public (incorrectly) believes it to be a "necessary evil" for medical progress. An article which appeared in the UK Guardian newspaper referred to a "public which doesn't necessarily understand the issues." This exemplifies the dangerous perception that researchers are the authority who should not and cannot be questioned. This unfortunate conclusion has allowed users of animals to continue their unethical and unscientific work unabated for too long. With such work being shrouded in secrecy, the public is denied access to knowing the truth of what is actually happening and are therefore not able to make an informed judgment, nor can they object accordingly.

Whilst researchers continue to use animals in medical research they are wasting precious resources—time and money—that should be used to find better, more ethical and scientifically-valid ways. Unfortunately however, whilst no one questions their methodology they will continue to work unopposed, backed by huge vested interests, constantly promising that their "miracle cures" are close by. If animal testing was banned tomorrow, research would not cease—that is not the nature of true science. Researchers would have no choice but to look further into alternatives.

Professional Opposition

Opposition to animal experiments is not limited to animal rights activists and people who just don't like cruelty to animals. It is now being acknowledged by medical professionals around the world as a dangerous and erroneous way to research human health.

The Medical Research Modernisation Committee (MRMC) is a national health advocacy group in the United States composed of physicians, scientists and other health care professionals who evaluate the benefits, risks and costs of medical research methods and technologies.

Founded in 1985, The Physicians Committee for Responsible Medicine (PCRM) is another US-based nonprofit organization that promotes preventive medicine, conducts clinical research, and encourages higher standards for ethics and effectiveness in research. It is comprised of doctors and laypersons working together for compassionate and effective medical practice, research, and health promotion.

Doctors and Lawyers for Responsible Medicine (DLRM) is based in the UK and was established in 1995 because of the need to inform the public about the dangers posed to human health arising from the misguided notion that medical progress is dependent on animal experiments.

EVALUATING THE AUTHOR'S ARGUMENTS:

According to viewpoint author Humane Research Australia, animal-based research has led to many mistakes and disasters. How do these examples affect your opinions on animal research? Could an article like this only choose examples that support its claims? What additional research would you need to do to support or counter this viewpoint?

Animal Testing Is Bad Science

People for the Ethical Treatment of Animals

"Ethics dictate that the value of each life in and of itself cannot be superseded by its potential value to anyone else."

In the following viewpoint, People for the Ethical Treatment of Animals (PETA) addresses some of the claims made in favor of animal testing. The authors argue that these claims are not true. They suggest that animal research is not necessary, and in fact has many downsides. The viewpoint claims that the practice only continues because it's hard to change an old habit. This viewpoint also argues that sacrificing animals for human benefit is not ethical. It states that animals suffer greatly from research experiments. Therefore, in this organization's opinion, there is never any reason to experiment on animals. PETA is an American animal rights organization.

AS YOU READ, CONSIDER THE FOLLOWING QUESTIONS:
1. Have animal experiments helped find cures for cancer, according to the viewpoint?
2. Compare this viewpoint's statements about the Animal Welfare Act to the claims in Chapter 1, Viewpoint 4. Are the claims of the two articles consistent?
3. Do medical students have to dissect animals?

S tudies published in prestigious medical journals have shown time and again that animal experimentation wastes lives— both animal and human—and precious resources by trying to infect animals with diseases that they would never normally contract. Fortunately, a wealth of cutting-edge non-animal research methodologies promises a brighter future for both animal and human health. The following are common statements supporting animal experimentation followed by the arguments against them.

"Every Major Medical Advance Is Attributable to Experiments on Animals"

This is simply not true. An article published in the esteemed Journal of the Royal Society of Medicine has even evaluated this very claim and concluded that it was not supported by any evidence. Most experiments on animals are not relevant to human health, they do not contribute meaningfully to medical advances, and many are undertaken simply out of curiosity and do not even pretend to hold promise for curing illnesses. The only reason people are under the misconception that these experiments help humans is because the media, experimenters, universities, and lobbying groups exaggerate the potential they have to lead to new cures and the role they've played in past medical advances.

"If We Didn't Use Animals, We'd Have to Test New Drugs on People"

The fact is that we already do test new drugs on people. No matter how many tests on animals are undertaken, someone will always be the first human to be tested on. Because animal tests are so unreliable, they make those human trials all the more risky. The National Institutes of Health (NIH) has noted that 95 percent of all drugs that are shown to be safe and effective in animal tests fail in human trials because they don't work or are dangerous. And of the small percentage of drugs approved for human use, half end up being relabeled because of side effects that were not identified in tests on animals.

Using blood and tissue samples from animals to make conclusions about humans might not always be the best method. There are many serious considerations, which makes the issue of animal testing quite complex.

"We Have to Observe the Complex Interactions of Cells, Tissues, and Organs in Living Animals"

Taking healthy beings from a completely different species, artificially inducing a condition that they would never normally contract, keeping them in an unnatural and stressful environment, and trying to apply the results to naturally occurring diseases in human beings is dubious at best. Physiological reactions to drugs vary enormously from species to species (and even within a species). Penicillin kills guinea pigs. Aspirin kills cats and causes birth defects in rats, mice, guinea pigs, dogs, and monkeys. And morphine, a depressant in humans, stimulates goats, cats, and horses. Further, animals in laboratories typically display behavior indicating extreme psychological distress, and experimenters acknowledge that the use of these stressed-out animals jeopardizes the validity of the data produced.

"Animals Help in the Fight Against Cancer"

Through taxes, donations, and private funding, Americans have spent hundreds of billions of dollars on cancer research since 1971. However, the return on that investment has been dismal. A survey of 4,451 experimental cancer drugs developed between 2003 and 2011 found that more than 93 percent failed after entering the first phase of human clinical trials, even though all had been tested successfully on animals. The authors of this study point out that animal "models" of human cancer created through techniques such as grafting human tumors onto mice can be poor predictors of how a drug will work in humans.

"Science Has a Responsibility to Use Animals to Keep Looking for Cures for All the Horrible Diseases that People Suffer From"

Every year in the U.S., animal experimentation gobbles up billions of dollars (including 40 percent of all research funding from the National Institutes of Health), and nearly $3 trillion is spent on health care. While funding for animal experimentation and the number of animals used in experiments continues to increase, the U.S. still ranks 42nd in the world in life expectancy and has a high infant mortality rate compared to other developed countries. A 2014 review paper co-authored by a Yale School of Medicine professor in the prestigious medical journal The BMJ documented the overwhelming failure of experiments on animals to improve human health. It concluded that "if research conducted on animals continues to be unable to reasonably predict what can be expected in humans, the public's continuing endorsement and funding of preclinical animal research seems misplaced."

"Many Experiments Are not Painful To Animals And Are Therefore Justified."

The only U.S. law that governs the use of animals in laboratories, the Animal Welfare Act (AWA), allows animals to be burned, shocked, poisoned, isolated, starved, forcibly restrained, addicted to drugs, and brain-damaged. No experiment, no matter how painful or trivial, is prohibited—and painkillers are not even required. Even when alternatives to the use of animals are available, U.S. law does not require that they be used—and often they aren't. Because the AWA specifically excludes rats, mice, birds, and cold-blooded animals, more than 95 percent of the animals used in laboratories are not even covered by the minimal protection provided by federal laws. Because they aren't protected, experimenters don't even have to provide them with pain relief.

Between 2010 and 2014, nearly half a million animals—excluding mice, rats, birds, and cold-blooded animals—were subjected to painful experiments and not provided with pain relief. A 2009 survey by researchers at Newcastle University found that mice and rats who underwent painful, invasive procedures, such as skull surgeries, burn experiments, and spinal surgeries, were provided with post-procedural pain relief only about 20 percent of the time.

"We Don't Want to Use Animals, but We Don't Have Any Other Options"

The most significant trend in modern research is the recognition that animals rarely serve as good models for the human body. Human

clinical and epidemiological studies, human tissue- and cell-based
research methods, cadavers, sophisticated high-fidelity human-patient
simulators, and computational
models have the potential to be more
reliable, more precise, less expensive,
and more humane alternatives to
experiments on animals. Advanced
microchips that use real human cells
and tissues to construct fully func-
tioning postage stamp–size organs
allow researchers to study diseases

and also develop and test new drugs to treat them. Progressive scientists have used human brain cells to develop a model "microbrain,"
which can be used to study tumors, as well as artificial skin and bone
marrow. We can now test skin irritation using reconstructed human
tissues (e.g., MatTek's EpiDermTM), produce and test vaccines using
human tissues, and perform pregnancy tests using blood samples
instead of killing rabbits.

Experimentation using animals persists not because it's the best
science but because of archaic habits, resistance to change, and a lack
of outreach and education.

"Don't Medical Students Have to Dissect Animals?"

Not a single medical school in the U.S. uses animals to train medical
students, and experience with animal dissection or experimentation
on live animals isn't required or expected of those applying to medical
school. Medical students are trained with a combination of sophisticated human-patient simulators, interactive computer programs, safe
human-based teaching methods, and clinical experience.

Today, one can even become a board-certified surgeon without
harming any animals. Some medical professional organizations, like
the American Board of Anesthesiologists, even require physicians to
complete simulation training—not animal laboratories—to become
board-certified.

"Animals Are Here for Humans to Use. If We Have to Sacrifice 1,000 or 100,000 Animals in the Hope of Benefiting One Child, It's Worth It."

If experimenting on one intellectually disabled person could benefit 1,000 children, would we do it? Of course not! Ethics dictate that the value of each life in and of itself cannot be superseded by its potential value to anyone else. Additionally, money wasted on experiments on animals is money that could instead be helping people, through the use of modern, human-relevant non-animal tests.

EVALUATING THE AUTHOR'S ARGUMENTS:

Viewpoint author PETA is a radical group in favor of animal rights. PETA's goal is to end all animal tests. Does knowing this background on the organization affect your opinion of the viewpoint? Compare this viewpoint to Chapter 1, Viewpoints 1 and 3. How can different people or groups consider a topic such as animal testing and come up with such wildly different claims?

Research Involving Animals Is Poorly Understood

"At least 75% of winners of the Nobel Prize in Medicine or Physiology used non-human animals in their research."

Gavan McNally

In the following viewpoint Gavan McNally argues that it is important to remember that animal testing has led to many important scientific and medical breakthroughs and continues to improve the lives of humans. The author admits that there are difficulties in animal testing but urges the reader to weigh these against the successes. McNally notes that there are many legislative regulations in place in Australia that keep the system in check. Gavan McNally is a professor of behavioral neuroscience at University of New South Wales in Australia.

AS YOU READ, CONSIDER THE FOLLOWING QUESTIONS:

1. What medical breakthrough is a success of animal research?
2. Why does the author note his "cautious" use of the word failure?
3. What is an example of animal research legal and regulatory framework in Australia?

A USTRALIANS SAY NO TO ANIMAL EXPERIMENTS," rang the headline of a recent media release by the activist group Humane Research Australia, referring to an opinion poll it commissioned in May that found:

> the majority of Australians are opposed to such an archaic practice and recognise the need to seek more humane and scientifically-valid options.

But research involving non-human animals remains poorly understood and highly emotive.

Perhaps the best single word response to Humane Research Australia's claims is: penicillin. Its application by scientists Howard Florey, Ernst Chain, Norman Heatley and their colleagues to treat bacterial infection in mice—then humans—highlights the difficulties and successes of animal research.

Studies in non-human animals have led to countless other treatments. Some examples include vaccinations, medications for high blood pressure, neuroprotective agents, deep brain stimulation for Parkinson's disease, antidepressants, analgesics, cardiac defibrillators, and pacemakers. These alleviate pain and suffering. They extend lifespans.

Along the way to these successes were numerous discoveries in basic science. The knowledge from basic research was central to advancement but appeared to add little to solving the pressing medical problems of the day. There were many blind alleys and apparent failure. (I use "failure" cautiously, as one scientist's noise is another's signal.)

Not Lost in Translation

Critics of animal research, and advocates of its abolition, focus heavily on failures in clinical translation and otherwise successful efforts in basic but incremental research.

Typically these criticisms invoke the very real difficulties of cross-species comparison, but draw the wrong conclusion. Species X differs from humans on variable Y; hence all work in species X is "scientifically invalid" and a "waste of resources".

The macaque monkey, shown in the wild in a Cambodian forest, is a common animal used in research.

Next, basic research is equated with "morbid curiosity". Often the ante is raised and science without clear translation to a human condition is portrayed as a flagrant waste of valuable resources.

Finally, misunderstood concepts such as "biological complexity" are invoked to explain why work in model preparations or in vitro systems is flawed.

When considering the merit of these criticisms, I suggest one looks towards Stockholm each year on December 10. At least 75% of winners of the Nobel Prize in Medicine or Physiology used non-human animals in their research.

But perhaps the most astonishing criticism is that there is no independent assessment, transparency, or accountability in animal research.

Legalities

All research involving animals occurs inside a legal and regulatory framework. Nationally, the Australian Code of Practise from the National Health and Medical Research Council provides one framework.

The fundamental principles are that researchers should act to reduce the number of animals used, refine their procedures to minimise impacts, and replace, wherever possible, animals with alternatives.

States have their own, but largely similar, acts and regulations. New South Wales, for example, has the Prevention of Cruelty to Animals Act 1979, Prevention of Cruelty to Animals Regulation 2012, Animal Research Act 1985, and Animal Research Regulation 2005. Victoria has the Prevention of Cruelty to Animals Act 1986 and the Prevention of Cruelty to Animals Regulations 2008.

Ethics Committees

Research institutions and their researchers are accredited, licensed, and authorised to conduct animal research. A condition is that the institution forms an Animal Care and Ethics Committee. These committees include researchers themselves, but also independent members such as lay members, representatives from animal welfare groups, and veterinarians. They consider applications from researchers, request significant revisions and approve or reject them.

The independent members are key drivers and promoters of animal welfare. They read and evaluate applications, force researchers to clearly justify the need for animal use, and frequently suggest refinements to reduce impact. Portraying these members as ineffectual and their contributions as "rubber stamps" is offensive and does them a great disservice.

The institution, its animal ethics committee and researchers are subject to inspections (such as the Animal Research Review Panel in NSW and Bureau of Animal Welfare in Victoria). These are conducted by dedicated and professional staff. They ensure regulatory compliance and continual improvement in animal welfare.

If research involves native species or fieldwork, then additional levels of independent assessment and approval (such as NSW Office for Environment and Heritage) are required.

Still Further Checks

There are other independent checks in this system. Most research requires funds, so researchers seek funding from independent agencies such as the National Health and Medical Research Council and the Australian Research Council. These funds are exceptionally hard-won. The idea that research funded via these agencies lacks significance and scientific excellence is absurd.

Opposition to animal research is conducted in many ways. At the extremes, activists invade laboratories, threaten researchers and firebomb their homes and cars. These acts are illegal. They fail to win opinion.

More moderate approaches include petitioning government and funding bodies to reduce or eliminate funding of animal research; and petitioning institutions about "wasteful" or inappropriate research.

Basic research is being carefully selected, misrepresented and trivialised in these campaigns.

These moderate strategies are designed to disrupt research and its administration, to influence policy, as well as to shift public opinion. They ought to be met and refuted.

EVALUATING THE AUTHOR'S ARGUMENTS:

Viewpoint author Gavan McNally argues that scientific research conducted on animals has led to important medical breakthroughs. Do you agree that attempts to oppose animal testing should be quieted by the regulation and system checks that are in place by the Australian government?

Animal Tests Don't Help Humans

Cruelty Free International

"We have cured mice of cancer for decades and it simply didn't work in human beings."

In the following viewpoint, Cruelty Free International argues that animal experiments often don't work. The authors note that humans and animals are different in many ways. Like previous viewpoints, this one lists statistics to show the failures of animal testing. It notes that nonhuman animals often react in ways humans do not. This leads to misleading test results. Cruelty Free International is an animal rights group that campaigns to stop all animal experiments. The group approves certain products as "cruelty free," meaning they have not been tested on animals.

AS YOU READ, CONSIDER THE FOLLOWING QUESTIONS:

1. What are some diseases that humans get, but animals do not get?
2. Are tests on some animals more successful then tests on other animals?
3. How can humans and other animals react differently to foods and drugs, according to the viewpoint?

"Arguments Against Animal Testing," Cruelty Free International. Reprinted by permission.

The harmful use of animals in experiments is not only cruel but also often ineffective. Animals do not get many of the human diseases that people do, such as major types of heart disease, many types of cancer, HIV, Parkinson's disease, or schizophrenia. Instead, signs of these diseases are artificially induced in animals in laboratories in an attempt to mimic the human disease. Yet, such experiments belittle the complexity of human conditions which are affected by wide-ranging variables such as genetics, socio-economic factors, deeply-rooted psychological issues and different personal experiences.

It is not surprising to find that treatments showing 'promise' in animals rarely work in humans. Not only are time, money and animals' lives being wasted (with a huge amount of suffering), but effective treatments are being mistakenly discarded and harmful treatments are getting through. The support for animal testing is based largely on anecdote and is not backed up, we believe, by the scientific evidence that is out there.

Despite many decades of studying conditions such as cancer, Alzheimer's disease, Parkinson's disease, diabetes, stroke and AIDS in animals, we do not yet have reliable and fully effective cures.

> *"The history of cancer research has been the history of curing cancer in the mouse. We have cured mice of cancer for decades and it simply didn't work in human beings."*
> *–Dr. Richard Klausner, former director of the US National Cancer Institute*

Unreliable Animal Testing

- 90% of drugs fail in human trials despite promising results in animal tests—whether on safety grounds or because they do not work
- Cancer drugs have the lowest success rate (only 5% are approved after entering clinical trials) followed by psychiatry drugs (6% success rate), heart drugs (7% success rate) and neurology drugs (8% success rate).
- Using dogs, rats, mice and rabbits to test whether or not a drug will be safe for humans provides little statistically useful insight,

our recent analysis found. The study also revealed that drug tests on monkeys are just as poor as those using any other species in predicting the effects on humans.

- Out of 93 dangerous drug side effects, only 19% could have been predicted by animal tests, a recent study found
- Using mice and rats to test the safety of drugs in humans is only accurate 43% of the time, a recent study found
- Out of 48 cancer drugs approved by the European Medicines Agency from 2009 to 2013 to treat 68 types of cancer, almost half showed no survival benefits according to a recent study. Even in cases where benefits were seen, the difference was judged to be 'clinically insignificant'.

Wasteful Animal Testing

- Despite the use of over 115 million animals in experiments globally each year, only 59 new medicines were approved in 2018 by the leading drug regulator, the U.S. Food and Drug Administration. Many of these are for rare diseases.
- The US drug industry invests $50 billion per year in research, but the approval rate of new drugs is the same as it was 50 years ago. Only 6% of 4,300 international companies involved in drug development have registered a new drug with the U.S. Food and Drug Administration since 1950.
- Even those drugs that are approved are not universally effective due to individual reactions—the top ten highest-grossing drugs in the USA only help between 1 in 4 and 1 in 25 people who take them
- Of over 1,000 potential stroke treatments that had been "successful" in animal tests, only approximately 10% progressed to human trials. None worked sufficiently well in humans.
- A review of 101 high impact basic science discoveries based on animal experiments found that only 5% resulted in approved treatments within 20 years.

Cancer researchers conducted tests in which a monkey was forced to smoke a cigarette to obtain water.

Dangerous Animal Testing

• Vioxx, a drug used to treat arthritis, was found to be safe when tested in monkeys (and five other animal species) but has been estimated to have caused around 320,000 heart attacks and strokes and 140,000 deaths worldwide.

• Human volunteers testing a new monoclonal antibody treatment (TGN1412) at Northwick Park Hospital, UK in 2006 suffered a severe allergic reaction and nearly died. Testing on monkeys at 500 times the dose given to the volunteers totally failed to predict the dangerous side effects.

• A recent drug trial in France resulted in the death of one volunteer and left four others severely brain damaged in 2016. The drug, which was intended to treat a wide range of conditions including anxiety and Parkinson's disease, was tested in four different species of animals (mice, rats, dogs and monkeys) before being given to humans.

• A clinical trial of Hepatitis B drug fialuridine had to be stopped because it caused severe liver damage in seven patients, five of whom died. It had been tested on animals first.

• Only one third of substances known to cause cancer in humans have been shown to cause cancer in animals.

• Animals do not get many of the diseases we do, such as Parkinson's disease, major types of heart disease, many types of cancer, Alzheimer's disease, HIV or schizophrenia.

• An analysis of over 100 mouse cell types found that only 50% of the DNA responsible for regulating genes in mice could be matched with human DNA.

• The most commonly used species of monkey to test drug safety (Cynomolgous macaque monkeys), are resistant to doses of paracetamol (acetaminophen) that would be deadly in humans.

• Due to the many important differences between monkeys and humans in brain structure and function, data collected from monkeys used in neuroscience research are misleading and of poor relevance to people, our recent analysis found.

- Chocolate, grapes, raisins, avocados and macadamia nuts are harmless in people but toxic to dogs.
- Aspirin is toxic to many animals, including cats, mice and rats and would not be on our pharmacy shelves if it had been tested according to current animal testing standards.

EVALUATING THE AUTHOR'S ARGUMENTS:

In this viewpoint, Cruelty Free International argues that animal testing should be stopped because it is not useful. Previous viewpoints have claimed that animal testing is unethical. Which argument has the most impact on your opinion of the subject? Why?

Chapter 3

What Are Alternatives to Animal Testing?

Many exciting technologies could make animal testing obsolete in the future.

Use Human Tissue Instead

Gareth Sanger and Charles Knowles

"It's clear that using human tissues reduces animal use."

In the following viewpoint, Gareth Sanger and Charles Knowles state that animal research is necessary. However, they argue that researchers should be using more alternatives. One alternative is using human tissues, which may be removed as a normal part of surgery and preserved for future use. They may also be used immediately after an operation. The latter may give better results, as the tissues haven't been frozen or put in a preservative. The authors argue that in many cases, the use of human tissue can be as accurate as that using live animals. Gareth Sanger is a professor of neuropharmacology at Queen Mary University of London. Charles Knowles is a clinical professor of surgical research at Queen Mary University of London.

AS YOU READ, CONSIDER THE FOLLOWING QUESTIONS:

1. Rodents can't vomit. How can this affect the results of animal tests?
2. Do patients need to give permission for the use of their tissue removed during surgery?
3. Why might researchers want to know some basic details about the patients donating tissue, such as their age and sex?

"Cut Down on Animal Testing by Building a Human Tissue Lab," by Gareth Sanger and Charles Knowles, The Conversation, July 29, 2013. https://theconversation.com/cut-down-on-animal-testing-by-building-a-human-tissue-lab-15525. Licensed under CC BY-ND 4.0.

A nimal testing is on the rise in the UK, according to Home Office figures. The figures suggest that the government's plan to reduce its use in scientific research hasn't been successful so far, and much of the increase may be due to an increase in genetically altered animals, primarily mice and fish.

But although animal research is still necessary to test new drugs before human trials, we're increasingly finding ways to test new substances on alternatives. This is important not just to reduce animal use but also to improve the quality of the science that is carried out for the benefit of human health.

Rodents Can't Vomit

Cells in our tissues recognise many substances, such as hormones or neurotransmitters—the chemicals that are released from nerves which control what the cell does, for example contracting a muscle cell.

To study the receptors that pick up these signals, we clone them and insert them into a "host cell" that can be easily grown in a lab. From there we can start to test new drugs and to see what effect they have on the living cell. To understand how the receptors, and the drugs we take, control wider body functions, the next step usually involves studying animals in laboratories—often rodents like rats, mice and guinea-pigs.

But human receptors in host cells don't always behave in the same way as they would in the body, which can give scientists misleading data. And some human receptors aren't found in rodents, or if they are, have different functions. This makes it difficult to properly predict the functions of the receptors and as a result, expensive clinical trials on new drugs can fail.

The gut is a good example: it has basic functions that are similar in both humans and other animals. But there are some surprising and remarkable differences. Most obvious is that rodents can't vomit.

Their guts also lack certain hormones found in humans, and different ones that respond to nausea-inducing stimuli. Certain receptors are structured differently and respond differently when given the same stimuli.

Rodents also possess a large caecum, which in humans has shrunk to become our appendix, and drugs and hormones have different functions in human and rodent intestines.

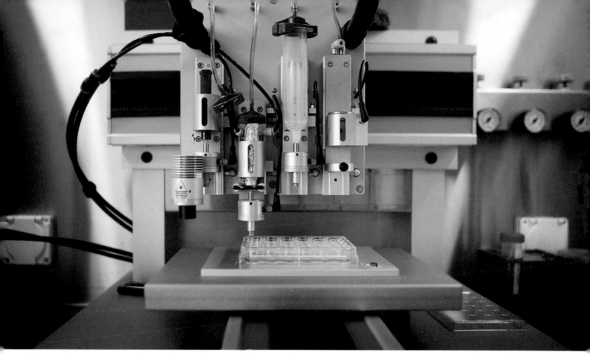

Bioprinters can produce 3D tissue that simulates human tissue in the body. This technology can reduce animal experiments in development of medications.

There's also an extraordinary variation between highly in-bred "strains" of laboratory mice, each of which is distinguished from the other by millions of small genetic variations—so the argument for uniformity isn't entirely true. And for each molecular change, who's to say which strain is more or less predictable than what happens in humans?

Setting Up a Human Tissue Lab

One solution to these problems is to study the functions of human tissues (removed as a normal part of surgery)—using human tissues to understand human disease. This improves both the quality of the science and reduces the numbers of animals used in research.

Changes in human tissue structures caused by disease are commonly studied and "banks" of tissues have been frozen or preserved for future use. But it's less common to study their functions when tissues have to be kept alive and studied almost immediately after being removed from the body.

To study human tissue functions requires clear collaboration between a whole host of medical staff, from surgeons, theatre staff, pathologists, scientists and also the patients themselves, who need to give their consent. And this is what we've been doing.

It's clear that using human tissues reduces animal use. Both directly—for example, up to 16 different preparations may be cut from a single human specimen in experiments looking at gastrointestinal muscle contractions, which requires four to eight different mice to achieve the same outcome—and indirectly, by demonstrating which animal experiments don't reflect what happens in humans and calling for an end to them.

Ethical Collection of Tissues

Tissues need to be collected and used ethically. Nearly all patients are happy for redundant surgical tissue to be used for research. However, the Alder Hey scandal in 1999, which involved the unauthorised removal and retention of human tissue, including children's organs, forced the international research community to tighten research rules.

Access to human tissue for research now requires ethics documentation and informed consent. It's standard practice to ensure there's no direct link between the tissue and the identity of the patient.

In our team, a "point person", operating on behalf of different scientists, ensures consent and liaises between the surgeon and pathologist. This means that tissues are promptly collected "fresh" from the operating theatre and are not placed in formalin, or formaldehyde, which is normal practice.

After a pathologist has dissected a research sample and taken all they need, we can then use it to carry out experiments.

Although the risk is low, there is always a possibility that the tissue has been removed from a patient with a transmissible infection. So scientists use special equipment to protect themselves from inhaling potentially contaminated aerosols from the nutrient solution the tissues are placed in and bubbled with oxygen to keep them alive.

Tissues from patients with known transmissible infections aren't collected.

Humans Vary Too

Mice vary. But so do humans—donors might be male or female and different ages. They might also enjoy a hedonistic or abstinent lifestyle. This means that when anyone claims that human tissue research is better than using laboratory animals, there is always the counterclaim that animal research is more precise, with fewer variables.

But variation can be reduced by surgical techniques that minimise damaging the tissue during removal. Collection of basic patient details (age, gender, disease, regular medications taken) and attention to other variables such as tissue recovery times, means human tissue research approaches the precision that is expected from animal studies.

EVALUATING THE AUTHOR'S ARGUMENTS:

In Chapter 2, some viewpoints claimed that methods such as tissue research are as good as animal testing. In Chapter 1, Viewpoint 5, the author argued that in vitro tests are not good enough. In this viewpoint, authors Gareth Sanger and Charles Knowles argue that in vitro tests are often as good as testing on animals, though not necessarily a full replacement. Can you reconcile these viewpoints? What claims influence you more, those by college professors or those by animal rights organizations? Why?

Computer Simulations Can Replace Animal Testing

Elisa Passini, Blanca Rodriguez, and Patricia Benito

"Computer simulations are a faster, cheaper and effective alternative to animal experiments."

In the following viewpoint, Elisa Passini, Blanca Rodriguez and Patricia Benito look at testing drugs for their effects on the heart. They argue that computer models can be more accurate than testing on animals when it comes to predicting harmful drug effects. Using these computer models could lead to safer drugs with fewer harmful side effects. The authors do not claim that all animal tests could be eliminated and replaced with computer models. However, they argue that computer models are more successful than animal testing in certain circumstances. In the future, computer models may be able to do even more. The authors are researchers at the University of Oxford.

AS YOU READ, CONSIDER THE FOLLOWING QUESTIONS:
1. How does the accuracy of computer models compare to animal testing in the specific example mentioned?
2. How quickly can computer models analyze the effects of a drug on a few heart cells?
3. How quickly can computer models simulate a heartbeat?

S afety is imperative before new medicines are given to patients—which is why drugs are tested on millions of animals worldwide each year to detect possible risks and side effects. But research shows computer simulations of the heart have the potential to improve drug development for patients and reduce the need for animal testing.

Animal testing has, to date, been the most accurate and reliable strategy for checking new drugs, but it is expensive, time consuming and—for some—highly controversial.

There is also the potential for some side effects to be missed due to the differences between animals and humans. Drug trials are particularly problematic for this reason and it's clear that new testing methods are needed to enable the development of better and safer medicines.

Humans and Other Animals

A variety of species of animals—including rats, mice, rabbits, guinea pigs, dogs and pigs—are used each year in drug development to predict the possible side effects for the heart in humans.

But while the underlying biology is similar, small differences between animal and human cells are amplified when a patient takes a drug. It means predicting the risk to patients is limited to an accuracy rate of around (75% to 85%), research shows, and it also leads to drug withdrawals from the market because of cardiovascular safety issues.

However, it's now possible to test a new heart drug in a "virtual human." Our recent research at the University of Oxford's Department of Computer Science demonstrates that computational models representing human heart cells show higher accuracy

The Living Heart Project is a virtual reality (VR) model of a human heart. Computer models of the heart are believed to be important breakthroughs in drug development.

(89-96%) than animal models in predicting an adverse drug effect, such as dangerous arrhythmias—where the heart beat becomes irregular and can stop.

It shows that human computational models would bring additional advantages by reducing the use of animal experiments in early stages of drug testing; improving drug safety, thereby lowering the risk for patients during clinical trials; and speeding up the development of medicines for patients in urgent need of healthcare.

Computer Models of the Heart

British biologist Denis Noble first began experimenting with computer models of the heart in Oxford in 1960. Since then, the technology has evolved and it is ready to be integrated into industrial and clinical settings.

Thanks to human experimental data, human computer models are now available at different scales, from single cells to whole hearts, and they can be used to explore the behaviour of the human heart in healthy or diseased conditions, and under drug action.

Instead of a one-model-fits-all method, there are also new population-based approaches. Everyone is different, and some drugs can have harmful side effects only for certain parts of the population, such as people with a specific genetic mutation or disease.

The study by the Computational Cardiovascular Science team demonstrated that human computer models of heart cells are more accurate than animal experiments at predicting the drug-induced side effects for the heart in humans. This research won an international prize because of its potential to replace animal testing in labs.

We incorporated the technology into software, dubbed Virtual Assay, which is easy for non-experts to use in modelling and simulations.

The software offers a simple user interface for Microsoft Windows in which a control population of healthy cardiac cells with specific properties, based on human data, can be built. It can then be used to run computer-simulated—known as in silico—drug trials, before analysing the results. The whole process is very quick: it takes under five minutes using a modern laptop to test one drug in a population of 100 human cardiac cell models.

Several pharmaceutical companies are already using and evaluating Virtual Assay, which is available with a free academic licence and can be used by clinicians and pharmaceutical companies.

This research is part of a wider move towards the integration of computer models for drug safety testing which includes the Comprehensive in vitro Proarrhythmia Assay initiative, promoted by the US Food and Drug Administration and other organisations.

Pushing Computer Science Boundaries

While simulations of heart cells can run in a few minutes, 3D computer models of the whole heart still require a huge amount of computational power. One heartbeat, for example, can take about three hours in a supercomputer with almost 1,000 processors.

We're now working on 3D simulations of the heart to explore drug cardiac safety and efficacy on a larger scale. It includes an exploration of diseased conditions, such as acute ischemia—where the blood flow in one of the arteries around the heart is obstructed. This research is also part of the European CompBioMed project to build computer models for the whole human body: a virtual human.

By bringing together academia, the pharmaceutical industry and regulatory agencies we hope to accelerate the uptake of human-based in silico methodologies for the evaluation of cardiac drug safety and efficacy.

Computer simulations are a faster, cheaper and effective alternative to animal experiments—and they will soon play an important role in the early stages of drug development.

EVALUATING THE AUTHOR'S ARGUMENTS:

Viewpoint authors Elisa Passini, Blanca Rodriguez, and Patricia Benito claim that computer models can be more accurate than animal testing. Do you think we will be able to replace all animal testing with computer models someday? Why or why not? If yes, what should we do in the meantime?

Practice on Models, Not Animals

"Scientific studies show that non-animal methods are much less expensive than animal labs, students enjoy them—and they work."

Good Medicine

In the following viewpoint, which was written in 1995, authors from *Good Medicine* noted that even then new products were replacing animal testing. This viewpoint looks particularly at human patient simulators. These have largely replaced animals as learning tools for healthcare students. Many skills can be taught with the simulators. They are expensive to buy, but the cost is offset by the fact that they can be used repeatedly for years. Simulators may be better teaching tools than using animals, and they don't take animal lives. Some lower-cost options use computer models and are designed for teaching specific skills. *Good Medicine* is the Physicians Committee's quarterly member magazine.

AS YOU READ, CONSIDER THE FOLLOWING QUESTIONS:
1. What procedures can be taught on a simulator?
2. How does a graphic computer simulator differ from a mannequin simulator?
3. Can students learn as well from a simulator as from practicing on animals?

"Non-animal teaching methods show their superiority." Good Medicine, 4(3), 10-11, Physicians Committee for Responsible Medicine (PCRM), (1995, Autumn). Reprinted by permission.

New products that replace live animal labs in medical training are rapidly entering the marketplace. The most impressive new systems incorporate computerized mannequins, complex graphics, and sophisticated operator controls in state-of-the-art patient simulators. Students learn both medical concepts and manual procedures on life-size, interactive equipment that provides the benefits of anatomical correctness, unlimited repetition, scheduling convenience, and variable "health" conditions that prepare students for actual practice.

The Human Patient Simulator was developed by the University of Florida College of Medicine to train anesthesiologists in routine and crisis situations. Its interactive technology provides a realistic learning experience that is adaptable for a wide range of health care practitioners, including medical students, residents, nurses, and medical engineers.

The simulator mannequin has palpable pulses, heart and lung sounds, twitch response to nerve stimulation, and, yes, even a body temperature. Trainees can monitor its heart rate, cardiac rhythms, cardiac output, and blood pressure. Equipped with interface software and an instructor's remote control, the simulator also gives accurate patient responses to over 60 different drugs, mechanical ventilation, and other medical therapies, and allows the instructor to introduce new conditions.

The simulator's drug recognition and response system is particularly useful for replacing animal laboratories in medical school. Some medical schools still use dogs or other animals as laboratory subjects as basic science courses, where students inject the animals with various drugs to observe the change in their blood pressure, respiration, heart rate, etc. The animals are generally killed with a fatal injection at the end of the lab. The simulator allows medical students to observe accurate responses to drugs predicated on human patients without wasting the lives of animals.

The simulator's interactive design allows it to be used with all anesthesia gas delivery systems and mechanical ventilators. It connects to standard monitoring system, including EKG, invasive and non-invasive blood pressure and pulse monitors, and even responds to equipment malfunctions.

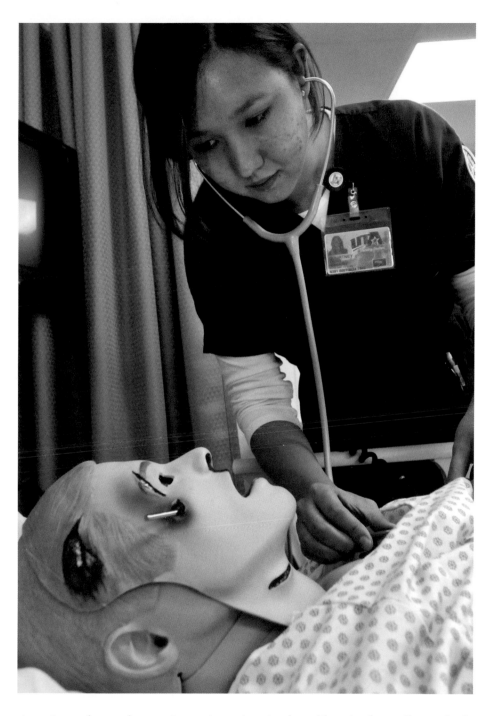

A nursing student works on an interactive patient simulator. These simulators allow medical and nursing students to be trained on mannequins that are very close to human beings.

Procedures that can be taught on the simulator include inserting artificial airways, taking non-invasive blood pressure measurements, monitoring arterial blood gases, and administering anesthesia. A special curriculum uses a series of clinical scenarios in which students manage the anesthesia and medications for a patient in a diabetic coma, surgical repair of an aortic aneurysm, treatment of end-stage renal disease, and other conditions.

The Human Patient Simulator has been used by the University of Florida system for over eight years. It sells for approximately $180,000, and has been purchased by, among other sites, Mount Sinai Anesthesia Simulation Center, the University of Rochester Strong Memorial Hospital, Vanderbilt University in Nashville, and Santa Fe Community College in Gainesville, where the Florida Department of Education has developed a simulator-based curriculum for health care professionals.

Another hands-on, interactive simulator is the Virtual Anesthesiology Training Simulation System, developed from research done by David Gaba and John Williams of Stanford University, and Howard Schwid of the University of Washington. Like the Human Patient Simulator, this product combines a life-size mannequin, computer systems, an operator's console, and monitoring equipment interface. It is appropriate for basic medical instruction in a variety of disciplines, as well as advanced training in anesthesia crisis management, emergency room care, critical care, and advanced cardiac life support.

This simulator is close to the Human Patient Simulator in design and application, and provides similar benefits. Some interesting features include mechanical lungs which ventilate spontaneously and can even simulate blockage of one lung, palpable carotid and radial pulses, points in the arm where intravenous fluids and drugs can be administered, a tongue swelling device, a color graphics workstation which serves as the operator's console, and an interface cart that connects the mannequin to the computers, monitors and anesthesia machine.

High-Tech, Not High-Priced

Want a high-quality simulator and don't have $180,000 in loose change? The Critical Care and Anesthesia Simulator programs offered by Anesoft Corporation offer real-time, graphic computer simulations that reproduce patient care in an Intensive Care Unit or an anesthesia environment for a fraction of the cost of a simulator with a mannequin. With the Critical Care Simulator, developed at the University of Washington, students manage twenty different critically ill patients by controlling their airway, ventilation, fluids and medications. The program reproduces the patient's monitors and simulates its responses, including those for boluses and infusions of about seventy drugs, which means it too can be used in place of the traditional dog lab. The simulated cases can be temporarily suspended to provide diagnostic and therapeutic information for optimum management of the clinical situation.

The Anesthesia Simulator Consultant reproduces dozens of anesthesia environments in real-time, including anaphylaxis, difficult airway, myocardial ischemia and pneumothorax. The simulated patient responds to management while an automated record-keeping system summarizes the case and an expert system provides immediate consultation. The Critical Care and Anesthesia Simulator software cost about $295 each.

Non-Animal Teaching Methods Show Their Superiority
Many medical schools have dropped old-fashioned animal labs. The non-animal methods are cheaper, they don't need to be anesthetized, and students don't object to them. But do they work?

The answer is a resounding yes. Emerging students show that non-animal methods teach as well or better than animal labs and save money in the bargain, not to mention the enormous savings in animal lives.

Researchers at the College of Veterinary Medicine in Auburn, Alabama, tested an interactive video system, assigning students to participate in either an animal laboratory or an interactive videodisc simulation. The two groups scored about the same on a multiple choice/short answer test, but the interactive video program was more time-efficient.

Instructors at the University of Chicago compared student responses to an animal laboratory versus a computer simulation, and found, "the students rated both highly, but the computer-based session received a higher rating." Patient-Oriented Problem Solving (POPS) is a small group teaching tool in which students solve clinical problems as a means of learning medical concepts. A study published by the Association of American Medical Colleges showed it to be effective in conveying principles of pharmacology, doing so at minimal cost.

Assisting in the operating room is the usual way that new surgeons learn their skills. However, some companies have pushed animal surgery laboratories in connection with sales of surgical products. Stephen M. Tsang, M.D., and his colleagues at Tulane University examined surgical complication and mortality rates for gallbladder surgery and found that those who had trained in animal laboratories performed no better than those who had not. In Dr. Tsang's words, "there is no need to attend an expensive and time-consuming classroom and animal laboratory course."

Pioneering heart surgeon Michael DeBakey said, "I gave up surgical training of our students and residents on animals years ago. We used to have a course. I stopped it completely. I said, "I'm not going to do this anymore on animals because we're going to put students in the operating room with humans." Dr. DeBakey went on to point out the ease of using non-animal methods. "You don't have to have a living animal to try to do microsurgery, say, to repair a vessel. You can use fresh cadavers. It's very easy. You just take a piece of tissue out of a fresh cadaver, whether it's an animal that died from some other reason or a human."

Okay, non-human teaching methods work. But will instructors or students find computer simulations, videos, or other methods to be as graphic and engrossing as a live animal laboratory? A method now being explored at Harvard Medical School may be just the answer to that question. Harvard recently allowed medical students to observe heart surgery in the hospital operating room rather than participate in an animal laboratory. In the operating room, a broad range of drugs are used in human patients—essentially the same drugs used in dog labs—and their effects on the cardiovascular system can be observed in great detail.

In support of this method, Robert Forstot, M.D., of the division of Cardiothoracic Anesthesia of Washington University in St. Louis, Missouri, wrote, "The demonstration of human pharmacology and physiology that is relevant to the needs of future physicians can be more appropriately achieved by taking medical students into the operating theater under the tutelage of staff anestheologists, rather than using dogs to demonstrate these drug effects. This is especially true if the students can be taken into the cardiac surgery suites, where I practice anesthesia."

In Dr. Forstot's words, the operating room is "an ideal venue from which to teach medical students both pharmacology and physiology that is relevant to their future practice."

Animal laboratories are obviously not essential to medical education, given that many medical schools have dropped them entirely. Happily, scientific studies show that non-animal methods are much less expensive than animal labs, students enjoy them—and they work.

EVALUATING THE AUTHOR'S ARGUMENTS:

This viewpoint argues that students learn as well or better on simulators as on animals. How does this relate to using animals to test drugs and medical treatments? Do you think simulators could work for that? Why or why not? In the time since this viewpoint was first published, the cost of human simulators has gone down anywhere from $750 to $75,000, depending on what they do. What else do you think has changed?

Reduce Suffering with the 3Rs

"Opinion polls of public attitudes consistently show that support for animal research is conditional on the 3Rs being put into practice."

NC3Rs

In the following viewpoint, NC3Rs goes into more detail on the 3Rs, first mentioned in Chapter 1. These guidelines have been adopted by many organizations. They have also affected international laws and laws in some countries. These guidelines are designed to reduce the number of animals used in experiments. In some cases, this includes replacing animal experiments with other research methods. The guidelines also attempt to reduce the pain and suffering of animals used in research. NC3Rs is a scientific organization based in the United Kingdom. It is dedicated to "replacing, refining and reducing the use of animals in research and testing."

AS YOU READ, CONSIDER THE FOLLOWING QUESTIONS:
1. What is "Replacement" as it relates to animal testing?
2. What is "Reduction" as it relates to animal testing?
3. What is "Refinement" as it relates to animal testing?

"The 3Rs", National Centre for the Replacement Refinement & Reduction of Animals in Research. Reprinted by permission. Accessed on September 24, 2019, https://www.nc3rs.org.uk/the-3rs.

The principles of the 3Rs (Replacement, Reduction and Refinement) were developed over 50 years ago providing a framework for performing more humane animal research. Since then they have been embedded in national and international legislation and regulations on the use of animals in scientific procedures, as well as in the policies of organisations that fund or conduct animal research. Opinion polls of public attitudes consistently show that support for animal research is conditional on the 3Rs being put into practice.

The NC3Rs is the UK's national organisation for the 3Rs. Our strategy is to advance the 3Rs by focusing on their scientific impacts and benefits. We have re-defined the standard 3Rs definitions so that they are more reflective of contemporary scientific practice and developments.

Definitions of the 3Rs

	Standard	Contemporary
Replacement	*Methods which avoid or replace the use of animals*	*Accelerating the development and use of models and tools, based on the latest science and technologies, to address important scientific questions without the use of animals*
Reduction	*Methods which minimise the number of animals used per experiment*	*Appropriately designed and analysed animal experiments that are robust and reproducible, and truly add to the knowledge base*
Refinement	*Methods which minimise animal suffering and improve welfare*	*Advancing research into animal welfare by exploiting the latest in vivo technologies and by improving understanding of the impact of welfare on scientific outcomes*

Replacement

Replacement refers to technologies or approaches which directly replace or avoid the use of animals in experiments where they would otherwise have been used.

For many years research animals have been used to answer important scientific questions including those related to human health. Animal models are often costly and time-consuming and depending on the research question present scientific limitations, such as poor relevance to human biology. Alternative models can address some of these concerns. In the last decade or so, advances in science and technology have meant that there are now realistic opportunities to replace the use of animals.

We divide replacement into two key categories, full and partial replacement.

Full replacement avoids the use of any research animals. It includes the use of human volunteers, tissues and cells, mathematical and computer models, and established cell lines.

Partial replacement includes the use of some animals that, based on current scientific thinking, are not considered capable of experiencing suffering. This includes invertebrates[1] such as Drosophila, nematode worms and social amoebae, and immature forms of vertebrates[2]. Partial replacement also includes the use of primary cells (and tissues) taken from animals killed solely for this purpose (i.e. not having been used in a scientific procedure that causes suffering).

Reduction

Reduction refers to methods that minimise the number of animals used per experiment or study consistent with the scientific aims. It is essential for reduction that studies with animals are appropriately designed and analysed to ensure robust and reproducible findings.

Reduction also includes methods which allow the information gathered per animal in an experiment to be maximised in order to reduce the use of additional animals. Examples of this include the

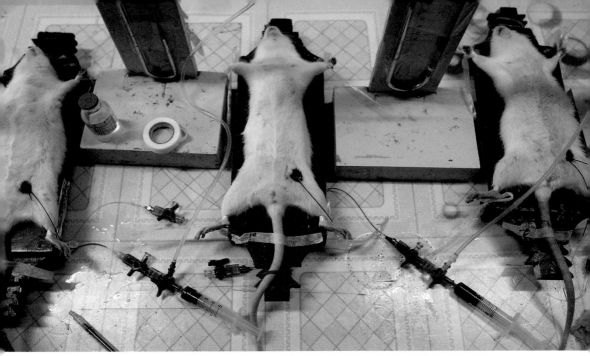

If animals are to be used for medical testing, the 3Rs must be employed. These are replacement, reduction, and refinement.

use of some imaging modalities which allow longitudinal measurements in the same animal to be taken (rather than for example culling cohorts of animals at specific time points), or microsampling of blood, where small volumes enable repeat sampling in the same animal. In these scenarios, it is important to ensure that reducing the number of animals used is balanced against any additional suffering that might be caused by their repeated use.

Sharing data and resources (e.g. animals, tissues and equipment) between research groups and organisations can also contribute to reduction.

Refinement

Refinement refers to methods that minimise the pain, suffering, distress or lasting harm that may be experienced by research animals, and which improve their welfare. Refinement applies to all aspects of animal use, from their housing and husbandry to the scientific procedures performed on them. Examples of refinement include ensuring the animals are provided with housing that allows the expression of species-specific behaviours, using appropriate anaesthesia and analgesia to minimise pain, and training animals to cooperate with procedures to minimise any distress.

Evidence suggests that pain and suffering can alter an animal's behaviour, physiology and immunology. Such changes can lead to variation in experimental results that impairs both the reliability and repeatability of studies.

We have recently published our strategy for improving animal welfare. (https://www.nc3rs.org.uk/news/strategy-improving-animal -welfare-and-quality-science)

Endnotes

1. Note cephalopods such as octopuses and squid are protected in the UK by the Animals (Scientific Procedures) Act 1986.

2. Under the UK's the Animals (Scientific Procedures) Act 1986 embryonic and fetal forms of mammals, birds and reptiles are protected during the last third of their gestation or incubation period, fish and amphibians once they can feed independently, and cephalopods at the point they hatch. Embryonic and fetal forms are protected from an earlier stage of development if they are going to live beyond the stage described above and the procedure is likely to cause them pain, suffering, distress or lasting harm after they have developed to that stage.

EVALUATING THE AUTHOR'S ARGUMENTS:

In this viewpoint NC3Rs promotes the 3Rs in animal testing. Do you think that following these guidelines does enough to prevent animal pain and suffering? Could more be done? Does the suffering of animals matter? How do you support your opinion?

Technological Innovations Are More Accurate and Relevant to Humans

"Non-animal research conducted using technological innovations have repeatedly proved to be more human-relevant and accurate than crude animal experiments."

PETA India

In the following viewpoint, PETA India argues that technology has surpassed the effectiveness of testing on animals. Because animal testing is cruel and nonconsensual, the authors assert. it is in everyone's best interest to take advantage of technological advances that better replicate human physiology without harming animals, such as in vitro testing, modelling, and microdosing. The authors explore several of these alternatives to animal testing that they say are more relevant and accurate to humans, even including human volunteers. PETA India works to save and improve the quality of life for animals.

AS YOU READ, CONSIDER THE FOLLOWING QUESTIONS:
1. On what species does India's Wildlife Protection Act prohibit experiments?
2. What are "organs-on-a-chip"?
3. Why might human simulators be more effective for surgical training?

The world's most forward-thinking scientists don't experiment on animals, because they know that other species' physiology differs from that of humans, so they can't accurately apply the results from experiments on animals to us. It's also cruel, wasteful, and unnecessary to subject animals to painful and deadly experiments, especially as superior technology that can replace animal testing already exists and is continuously being developed.

India has some laws to protect animals from experimentation: The Wildlife (Protection) Act, 1972, fully prohibits experiments on frogs, a protected species, and The Prevention of Cruelty to Animals Act, 1960, mandates that experiments on animals be avoided whenever possible. PETA India's scientists use their expertise to work to convince authorities that animal experiments can always be avoided.

Non-animal research conducted using technological innovations have repeatedly proved to be more human-relevant and accurate than crude animal experiments. Here are just a few examples of the available non-animal research methods and their benefits:

In Vitro Testing

In vitro tests allow researchers to predict more accurately how drugs, chemicals, cosmetics, and other consumer products will affect humans.

Harvard's Wyss Institute created "organs-on-chips" that contain human cells grown in an advanced system to mimic the structure and function of human organs and organ systems so that experimenters can use chips instead of animals for drug and toxicity testing and disease research. These chips can replicate diseases, drug responses, and human physiology more accurately than archaic animal experiments

Researchers at cruelty-free cosmetics companies are testing on vitro-grown reconstructed human skin instead of animals.

do, and some companies have already turned them into products that other researchers can use instead of animals.

Rather than injecting animals with substances or applying them to animals' shaved skin to test for allergic responses, CeeTox, Inc, developed a non-animal skin allergy test for cosmetics, medical device extracts, and other substances. MatTek's EpiDerm™—a human cell-based, 3-dimensional tissue model that replicates key traits of normal human skin—can replace animals in product development, regulatory testing, and basic exploratory research applications.

Meanwhile, EpiSkin has created 3-dimensional eye models. According to the company, "The reconstructed tissue forms a stratified and well-organised epithelium which is structurally, morphologically and functionally similar to the human cornea with the presence of basal, wing and mucus production cells." This technology can successfully replace rabbits and other animals in tests and in basic and applied biomedical research methods.

In 2016, the Ministry of Health and Family Welfare amended the Drugs and Cosmetics Act to replace animal tests with in vitro,

Organisation for Economic Co-operation and Development–validated tests, including skin and eye irritation and corrosion tests using 3-dimensional reconstructed models.

Computer (In Silico) Modelling

Another humane alternative to experimenting on animals is using in silico, or computational, models for toxicity prediction, which can provide information regarding the hazard potential of chemicals. These methods include databases to retrieve toxicological data as well as quantitative structure-activity relationships (QSARs), which can identify hazard potential. QSARs are increasingly being relied on in chemical testing.

Human-Patient Simulators

Human-patient simulators are strikingly lifelike, high-tech tools that offer hands-on medical training without harming animals.

TraumaMan replicates a breathing and bleeding human torso, complete with realistic layers of skin and tissue, ribs, and internal organs to train doctors to perform life-saving surgical procedures on patients with traumatic injuries. This state-of-the-art simulator is portable, less costly than animal-based exercises, and reusable. Studies show that doctors who learn these surgical skills using modern simulators are as proficient or more so than those who cut into animals, largely because simulators accurately mimic human anatomy, whereas dogs and pigs do not.

The Armed Forces Medical College is one example of a facility using a human-patient simulator. The tool can replicate life-threatening situations, including polytrauma, cardiac and respiratory emergencies, and more.

Help from Human Volunteers

Human volunteers have always been, and will always be, invaluable assets to the scientific community and to the progression of human medicine.

Advanced brain imaging and recording techniques—such as functional magnetic resonance imaging (fMRI)—with human volunteers can replace archaic, invasive brain experiments on animals.

Researchers are also using a method called "microdosing"—giving human volunteers an extremely small one-time drug dose and using sophisticated imaging techniques to monitor how the substance behaves in the body—to generate crucial information on a drug's safety and metabolism in humans before large-scale human trials. Microdosing replaces certain tests on animals and helps identify drug compounds that don't work in humans so that they won't needlessly advance to government-required testing on animals.

EVALUATING THE AUTHOR'S ARGUMENTS:

In this viewpoint PETA India argues that technological alternatives should replace animal testing. The authors support their argument by using both moral and results-oriented reasoning, claiming that animal testing is cruel and also that it is not as effective as testing using advanced technologies. Which strategy is more persuasive to you?

Facts About Animal Testing

Editor's note: These facts can be used in reports to add credibility when making important points or claims.

According to estimates, more than 115 million animals are used in laboratory experiments worldwide each year.

In the U.S., over 800,000 animals protected by the Animal Welfare Act (AWA) are used in research. The numbers are not tracked for mice, rats, fish, or birds, which make up 95 percent of animals used in experiments. Including these could bring the number of animals used in research in the U.S. to 12 million or more.

Guinea pigs, rabbits, hamsters, mice, and rats are common animals used in labs. Dogs, cats, and primates are also used in research. About 60,000 monkeys are used for experiments each year in the United States, Europe, and Australia.

The World Medical Association (WMA) states, "Animal use in biomedical research is essential for continued medical progress. The WMA Declaration of Helsinki requires that biomedical research involving human subjects should be based, where appropriate, on animal experimentation, but also requires that the welfare of animals used for research be respected."

The principles of the 3Rs are Replacement, Reduction and Refinement. These guidelines were developed as a framework for performing more humane animal research. Replacement refers to finding other methods of testing, which do not require animals. Reduction means using the fewest possible number of animals. Refinement means using methods that minimize animal suffering and improve their welfare.

The main U.S. federal law that regulates the treatment of animals in research is the Animal Welfare Act. The first version of the AWA was signed into law in 1966. The Animal Welfare Act provides the minimum acceptable standards for the treatment and care of certain animals. Not all animals are covered by the AWA. Other laws, policies, and guidelines may cover additional species, or further address animal care and use.

Sixty percent of all animals used in testing are used in biomedical research and product-safety testing. Biomedical research looks for ways to prevent and treat diseases in people and in animals. Product-safety research tests products to make sure they are safe for their intended use. Federal law requires manufacturers and importers to test many consumer productsto prove they follow safety requirements.

Alternatives to Animal Testing

"In vitro" refers to a process taking place outside a living organism. In vitro studies typically use a test tube or culture dish. Tests using human cells and tissue models can be used to assess the safety of drugs, chemicals, and consumer products. For example, human lung cells may be exposed to chemicals to test the health effects of inhaled substances. "Organs-on-chips" use human cells to mimic the structure and function of human organs and organ systems.

In silico is short for "in silicon," referring to the use of silicon in computer chips. The term refers to biological experiments using computers. Some computer models try to mimic human biology and the progression of developing diseases. They may also judge a substance's likelihood of being hazardous by comparing it to existing substances. According to PETA, "Studies show that these models can accurately predict the ways that new drugs will react in the human body and replace the use of animals in exploratory research and many standard drug tests."

Microdosing tests how a drug is metabolized in humans. Volunteers get one very small dose of the drug. Imaging techniques monitor how the drug behaves in the body. Microdosing can help screen out drug compounds that won't work in humans.

Human-Patient Simulators are lifelike computerized models. They may breathe, talk, bleed, convulse, and even "die." These models are used to teach medical and emergency response students. They have largely replaced the use of animals in medical training. Available models include infants, children, women, and men. Some are designed for specific skills training, such as delivering a child or treating severe trauma.

Arguments Against Animal Research

- Animal testing is cruel and inhumane. It is unethical to harm or kill animals, because they cannot give their consent to the experiment.
- Animals don't respond to drugs the way humans do, so animal research is often flawed and even dangerous for people. It can lead to the approval of harmful drugs. It can also mean potential cures are missed.
- Animal research is sometimes done simply out of curiosity and does not lead to cures for human health problems.
- Even after animal testing, we must test drugs on humans. Many drugs shown to be safe and effective in animal tests fail in human trials.
- Animal research is unnecessary, because we have suitable alternatives. Animal tests are more expensive than other methods, wasting research money as well as animal lives.

Arguments in Support of Animal Research

- Animal testing has contributed to many life-saving cures and treatments. Science has a responsibility to cure human diseases, and animal experiments are necessary for this.
- It is better to sacrifice an animal than a human. Besides, far more animals are killed for food than are used in research.
- It is acceptable to experiment on animals that are not closely related to humans, or on animals that we believe do not feel pain.
- Many experiments are not painful, and animals in labs are generally treated well. Laws and regulations protect animals from mistreatment.
- We need complex, living animals to see how whole systems react. Alternatives to animal research are not always as good.

Organizations to Contact

The editors have compiled the following list of organizations concerned with the issues debated in this book. The descriptions are derived from materials provided by the organizations. All have publications or information available for interested readers. The list was compiled on the date of publication of the present volume; the information provided here may change. Be aware that many organizations take several weeks or longer to respond to inquiries, so allow as much time as possible for the receipt of requested materials.

The American Association for Accreditation of Laboratory Animal Care (AAALAC) International

5205 Chairman's Court, Suite 300
Frederick, Maryland 21703
(301) 696-9626
email: accredit@aaalac.org
website: www.aaalac.org

AAALAC International is a nonprofit organization that promotes the humane treatment of animals in science. It provides voluntary assessment and accreditation programs.

Cruelty Free International

16a Crane Grove
London N7 8NN
United Kingdom
44-20-7700-4888
email: info@CrueltyFreeInternational.org
website: www.crueltyfreeinternational.org

Cruelty Free International is an animal rights group that campaigns to stop all animal experiments. The group approves certain products as "cruelty free," meaning they have not been tested on animals.

Doctors and Lawyers for Responsible Medicine (DLRM)
PO BOX 302
London N8 9HD
email: dlrm@gn.apc.org
website: www.dlrm.org
DLRM states as its objective "the immediate and unconditional abolition of all animal experiments, on medical and scientific grounds."

Humane Research Australia (HRA)
PO Box 517, Heathmont
Vic. 3135, Australia
61-1800-486-263
email: info@humaneresearch.org.au
website: www.humaneresearch.org.au
HRA "challenges the use of animal experiments and promotes more
humane and scientifically-valid non animal methods of research."

The Humane Society of the United States
1255 23rd Street NW, Suite 450
Washington, DC 20037
(202) 452-1100 or (866) 720-2676
contact form: www.humanesociety.org/forms/contact-us
website: www.humanesociety.org/
The Humane Society works to end all forms of animal cruelty. The
website includes information on ending cosmetics animal testing.

The Medical Research Modernisation Committee (MRMC)
3200 Morley Road
Shaker Heights, OH 44122
(216) 283-6702
contact form: www.mrmcmed.org/join.html
website: www.mrmcmed.org
MRMC is a national health advocacy group composed of physicians,
scientists, and other health care professionals "who evaluate the benefits, risks and costs of medical research methods and technologies."

The National Anti-Vivisection Society (NAVS)
53 W. Jackson Boulevard, Suite 1552
Chicago, IL 60604
(312) 427-6065
website: www.navs.org
NAVS is a nonprofit animal welfare organization based in London "dedicated to ending harmful, flawed and costly animal experiments through the advancement of smarter, human-relevant science."

National Centre for the Replacement Refinement & Reduction of Animals in Research (NC3Rs)
Gibbs Building, 215 Euston Road
London, NW1 2BE
email: enquiries@nc3rs.org.uk
website: www.nc3rs.org.uk/
NC3Rs is a scientific organization based in the United Kingdom. It is dedicated to "replacing, refining and reducing the use of animals in research and testing."

People for the Ethical Treatment of Animals (PETA)
501 Front Street
Norfolk, VA 23510
(757) 622-7382
contact form: www.peta.org/about-peta/contact-peta/email-form/
website: www.peta.org
The largest animal rights organization in the world, PETA focuses on the use of animals in laboratories, in the food industry, in the clothing trade, and in the entertainment industry.

The Physicians Committee for Responsible Medicine (PCRM)
5100 Wisconsin Avenue NW, Suite 400
Washington, DC 20016-4131
(202) 686-2210
contact form: www.pcrm.org/contact/research
website: www.pcrm.org
PCRM is a US-based nonprofit organization. Its goals include encouraging higher standards for ethics and effectiveness in research.

For Further Reading

Books

Gluck, John P. *Voracious Science and Vulnerable Animals: A Primate Scientist's Ethical Journey* (Animal Lives). Chicago, IL: University of Chicago Press, 2016. The author relates his journey from working in a primate lab to becoming a vocal activist for animal protection.

Herrmann, Kathrin. *Animal Experimentation: Working Towards a Paradigm Change* (Human-animal Studies). Leiden, Netherlands: Brill, 2019. The author is a veterinarian and expert on animal welfare with a focus on the 3Rs of animal experimentation.

Linzey, Andrew and Clair Linzey. *The Palgrave Handbook of Practical Animal Ethics* (The Palgrave Macmillan Animal Ethics Series). London, UK: Palgrave Macmillan, 2018. An in-depth examination of the issues and practices relating to animal ethics. Topics include animal experimentation, zoos, and farming.

Monamy, Vaughan. *Animal Experimentation: A Guide to the Issues.* Cambridge, UK: Cambridge University Press, 2017. An introduction to the controversy surrounding the use of animals in scientific research, product testing, and education. It discusses both the benefits and moral objections to the use of animals in research.

Newton, David. *The Animal Experimentation Debate: A Reference Handbook* (Contemporary World Issues). Santa Barbara, CA: ABC-CLIO, 2013. This book examines the debates over animal research from antiquity to the present day.

Pacelle, Wayne. *The Humane Economy: How Innovators and Enlightened Consumers Are Transforming the Lives of Animals.* New York, NY: William Morrow Paperbacks; Reprint edition, 2017. A leader of the Humane Society describes how businesses can end the suffering of animals.

Stewart, Tracy. *Do Unto Animals: A Friendly Guide to How Animals Live, and How We Can Make Their Lives Better.* New York, NY: Artisan, 2015 A former veterinary technician shares how people can help animals lead better lives.

Periodicals and Internet Sources

Capaldo, Theodora, "Animal Data Is Not Reliable for Human Health Research (Op-Ed)," Live Science, June 6, 2014. https://www.live-science.com/46147-animal-data-unreliable-for-humans.html

Hugo, "Animals Have Rights Just like Us," Youth Voices, January 27, 2017. https://www.youthvoices.live/2017/01/27/animals-have-rights-just-like-us/

Jones, Richard, "Could we upload a brain to a computer – and should we even try?" The Conversation, July 5, 2016. https://theconversation.com/could-we-upload-a-brain-to-a-computer-and-should-we-even-try-61928

Kretzer, Michelle, "Experiments on Animals Fail 90% of the Time. Why Are They Still Done?" People for the Ethical Treatment of Animals, January 31, 2018. https://www.peta.org/blog/experiments-on-animals-fail-90-of-the-time-why-are-they-still-done/

Lin, Doris, "Historical Timeline of the Animal Rights Movement," Thought Co. October 24, 2019. https://www.thoughtco.com/historical-timeline-of-animal-rights-movement-127594

Logue, Megan, "Animal Testing: Inhumane And Ineffective," Odyssey, September 21, 2015. https://www.theodysseyonline.com/animal-testing-inhumane-ineffective

McCaffrey, Suzanne, "Computerized Mannequins A New Era in Medical Training," Good Medicine, Autumn 1995. https://www.jivdaya.org/computerized_mannequins_a_new_era_medical_trainning.html

McKie, Robin, "Scientists told to stop wasting animal lives," Guardian, April 18, 2015. https://www.theguardian.com/science/2015/apr/18/animal-lives-wasted-in-drugs-safety-tests

Medawar, Sir Peter, "Welfare of Animals Used in Scientific Testing and Research Universities," Federation for Animal Welfare. https://www.ufaw.org.uk/why-ufaws-work-is-important/welfare-of-animals-used-in-scientific-testing-and-research

Mellon, Monica, "Animal testing is cruel and unreliable," Temple News, January 23, 2018. https://temple-news.com/animal-testing-is-cruel-and-unreliable/

People for the Ethical Treatment of Animals, Inc., "Animal Testing 101," PETA. https://www.peta.org/issues/animals-used-for-experimentation/animal-testing-101/

Pugh, Cheraine, "Animal Testing is Animal Cruelty," One World Education, Inc. https://www.oneworldeducation.org/animal-testing-animal-cruelty.

Understanding Animal Research, "Animal testing and the Safety of Medicines Bill 2010," Understanding Animal Research. http://www.understandinganimalresearch.org.uk/files/5714/1041/1545/Safety_of_Medicines_Bill_Jan_2012.pdf

Unknown, "Human Organs-on-Chips," Wyss Institute. https://wyss.harvard.edu/technology/human-organs-on-chips/

Unknown, "Using Research Organisms to Study Health and Disease," U.S. Department of Health and Human Services. https://www.nigms.nih.gov/education/Documents/ResearchOrg.pdf

Websites

AnimalResearch.info (www.animalresearch.info/) This site gives information about "when and why it is appropriate to use animals, and the history of this area of research." Articles explore some medicines based on animal research.

Animal Welfare Information Center—USDA (www.nal.usda.gov) The Animal Welfare Act mandates this center to provide information on improving animal care and use in research, testing, and teaching. The site covers laws and guidelines related to animal testing.

Johns Hopkins University Center for Alternatives to Animal Testing (CAAT) (caat.jhsph.edu/) This group focuses on alternatives to animal testing. Learn about programs, events, publications, and resources.

Kids4Research (kids4research.org) This website shows how scientists use animals in research. Watch videos of professionals talking about their jobs or take a video tour of an animal research facility. Find games and activities and learn about careers in research.

Index

A

acetaminophen, 76

acquired immunodeficiency syndrome (AIDS), 13, 14, 73

Akhtar, Aysha, 24, 26

Alzheimer's disease, 73, 76

anemia, 53

Anesthesia Simulator Consultant, 93

anesthetics, 19, 55, 92

Animal Research Act 1985, 70

Animal Research Regulation 2005, 70

Animal Research Review Panel, 70

animal rights movement, history of, 8

animal testing
  alternatives to, 9, 14–16, 42–47, 64–65, 79–83, 84–88, 89–90, 92–95, 101–105
  arguments against, 8, 42–47, 48–49, 51–59, 60–61, 63–66, 72–74, 76–77, 79–83, 96–100
  arguments for, 9, 11–17, 18–19, 21–22, 23–24, 26–27, 35–40, 67–71
  efficacy of, 42–47, 48–49, 51–59, 60–61, 63–66, 72–74, 76–77, 85–86, 93–95, 101–105

Animal Welfare Act, 8, 28–34, 64

anti-depressants, 54, 68

anti-diarrhea medication, 53

apes, compared to monkeys, 11, 14

arrhythmias, 86

arthritis, 54, 76

aspirin, 52, 63, 76

asthma, 54

Australian Code of Practice, 69

autism, 35–40

Autism's False Prophets, 36, 40

B

Benito, Patricia, 84–88

benzene, 52

Bernard, Claude, 51

birds, 21, 29, 31, 32, 64

blood pressure, 53, 68, 92

blood transfusions, 49, 52

bonobos, 14

brain injuries, 19

breast cancer, 19, 54

Bureau of Animal Welfare, 70

C

calcium supplements, 7

California Biomedical Research Association, 19

cardiac valves, 19

cats, 29, 31, 32, 33, 46, 52, 63, 76, 77

Picture Credits

Cover Oleksandr Lysenko/Shutterstock.com; p. 10 Siqui Sanchez/ The Image Bank/Getty Images; p. 13 George Steinmetz/Corbis Documentary/Getty Images; p. 20 Mauro Fermariello/Science Photo Library/Getty Images; p. 25 picture alliance/Getty Images; p. 30 Alexander Demianchuk/TASS/Getty Images; p. 38 Environment Images/Universal Images Group/Getty Images; p. 41 Eric Préau/ Sygma/Getty Images; p. 44 Yves Forestier/Sygma/Getty Images; p. 50 Leonard McCombe/The LIFE Picture Collection/Getty Images; p. 62 Daniel J. Cox/Oxford Scientific/Getty Images; p. 69 Aldar Darmaev/Alamy Stock Photo; p. 75 David Hiser/The Image Bank/ Getty Images; p. 78 NurPhoto/Getty Images; p. 81 BSIP/Universal Images Group/Getty Images; p. 86 The Boston Globe/Getty Images; p. 91 Fort Worth Star-Telegram/Tribune News Service/Getty Images; p. 99 China Photos/Getty Images; p. 103 Jean-Philippe Ksiazek/ AFP/Getty Images.